Killed by a Silver Bull

Killed by a Silver Bull

A Little Old Ladies' Mystery

Jo Lauer

DEDICATION

To all (especially little old ladies) who enjoy a good cozy mystery.

ACKNOWLEDGMENTS

Robbi Sommers Bryant, editor extraordinaire; Sue Spight, collaborator, beta reader, and all-around support person; Alice White and Lori Ubell, beta readers; Terry Freese, researcher; Michelle Fairbanks, cover artist; Leo Baquero, book formatting. Thank you, village.

Chapter 1

Whoomph!

"Help me up, please," Amanda groaned.

"Good God! I didn't think you'd actually *do* it." Marion bent down and offered a hand to Amanda who lay splayed on the ground atop a layer of hay.

It was early August, and the Sonoma County Fair was in bloom. The stinging summer heat did little to diminish the boundless energy of the fair-goers.

The crowd clapped and hooted as Amanda, with a lopsided grin, found her footing.

"Whatever possessed you to get on a mechanical bull?" Marion fussed about, brushing hay from Amanda's shirt and jeans.

"It was an impulse," Amanda said. She blinked and rolled her shoulders. "I can't quite explain it." She picked up her straw cowboy hat and whacked it against her thigh to dislodge dust from both.

At sixty-something, Amanda's impulsive streak still got her in trouble—only months ago she'd fallen in lust with her art teacher—with a near-fatal conclusion.

"Let's go check out the rest of the fair," Marion suggested. She pulled Amanda into the crowd.

The Ferris wheel whirled, and a rocket ride had stopped—upside-down riders laughing and waving. At the roller coaster, Amanda grabbed her stomach with both hands and said, "I think I've had my ride for the evening." She took Marion's elbow and steered her toward a row of games.

Tired, dusty men hawked their games with sloth-like enthusiasm: ball toss, shooting galleries, water targets, fish.

"Ah, this is more like it," Amanda said as she put her money down and picked up three darts. The first two missed the target. "Just warming up," she said. The third dart hit dead center. "Ha! Bullseye!" she yelled.

"I'll meet you in the Arts and Crafts building when you're done." Marion eyed the row of games she knew would entice Amanda. "Half hour?"

"Yeah, yeah, okay," Amanda said over her shoulder. She turned back to choose her prize, a fuzzy black bull.

Crossing the midway, Marion approached two boys fighting over cotton candy. The older boy, the space between his front teeth giving his sneer an amusing quality, shoved the younger boy, grabbed his paper cone, and turned to run away. Instead, he bumped right into Marion.

"Shame on you, you little bully!" she said. She grabbed the kid by the shoulders, spun him around, and said, "Give it back. Now." Stunned, he gave the cone back to the smaller boy whose tears balanced in the corners of his eyes.

"Thanks, lady." He grinned at her like a sweet cherub.

A former elementary school teacher, Marion's jaw still locked when she saw a child bullied. Back then, she was mandated to "redirect" the bully's behavior. *Redirect, my ass*, she thought now as she stood, hands planted on hips.

"No fair!" cried the older boy. "He took it from *me*. I'm telling mom." He stomped away in a fury.

So much for trying to help, Marion thought as she picked pink, spun sugar from her sleeve.

Amanda found Marion slumped on a bench outside the Arts and Crafts building. She looked like a wilted piece of lettuce in her light-green jumpsuit.

"Let's eat," they both said in unison.

The food aisles offered the standards: tacos, hot dogs, hamburgers, churros, ice cream, garlic fries.

3

"That's it!" Amanda said. She stopped short and pointed to a sign: Mom's Home Cooking. Amanda, whose parents neither cooked nor knew how to raise a child, took off at a trot toward the stand.

"Gosh, look Marion . . . real American food."

They stood together reading the menu board: grilled cheese sandwich, cup-o-soup, SpaghettiOs, fried bologna sandwich, tuna melt, fries, Jell-O, fish sticks. The list went on.

"I'm pretty sure they misspelled bologna," Amanda offered. "Doesn't it end in a 'Y?'"

"No, they got that right," Marion replied. "What an odd menu."

Amanda stepped up and placed her order. "I'll have a fried bologna sandwich please." She articulated each syllable. ". . . and some fries."

Marion stuck with soup and a childhood favorite, grilled cheese. The women made their way to a weathered picnic table.

Amanda set her stuffed bull on the table.

"Is that your grand prize?' Marion motioned toward the stuffed animal.

"He's guarding our food." Amanda unwrapped her sandwich. "See anything interesting in the Arts and Crafts?" Grease dripped down her chin.

Out of habit, Marion leaned forward and caught the bead of grease in her paper napkin.

"Actually, I did. There's a new category for arts this year—ink stamping. Some pieces were rather creative."

"Gee, sounds like a thrill." Amanda rolled her eyes. "Bet there's a long line to sign up for *that* class." She chuckled.

Marion shook her head as she scanned the fairground. "I think I've had about as much fun as I can handle for one day. Can we call it quits?" She dropped her trash into a large bin guarded by a fat bumble bee.

Amanda tossed hers over her shoulder and missed the can by a good foot. She tried again. Missed. Her next shot bounced off the rim to the ground.

"Oh, for God's sake," Marion sputtered. She picked up the wrappings and threw them into the trash.

Chapter 2

Several days later, Amanda sat at the kitchen table dressed in a fluorescent green jogging suit. Her gray hair, streaked with pink, was tied in pigtails and secured with orange yarn. Fire-engine red Nikes cradled her feet. The black check on the sides of the shoes was a must-have. Did she worry others might think her clothes unseemly for an older woman? She most certainly did not.

She inched her legs into a stretch and flexed her knees, one at a time, after her morning jog. *The Daily Advance* was spread in front of her. When the obituary page took up more space than the news, Amanda referred to the paper as *The Daily Decline*.

"*Tsk, tsk.* An eighty-year-old woman died of an apparent heart attack," she paraphrased from an article on the third page.

Marion cocked her head. "Why did that catch your eye? Do we know her?" She bustled around the kitchen making lunch. Marion, also in her late-sixties, had put on a few pounds since moving in with Amanda. With her gray hair in a bun and red-and-yellow apron, she resembled Mrs. Butterworth.

"Audrey Cuthbert. Don't know her. The only 'survived by' listed is a nephew who lives in Florida. She must have lived—and died—alone." Amanda slumped in her chair.

They exchanged a sorrowful look. "If we hadn't moved in together . . . there but for the grace might go either of us," Marion said.

Amanda nodded, folded the paper, and set it aside.

"*No!*" Marion said.

"No, what?" Amanda asked.

"'No what,' what?" Marion said.

"You said, a very emphatic 'no.'"

"I didn't say a thing," Marion said.

Amanda studied Marion's face. "Are you hearing things again?"

"Perhaps. I felt a vapor pass through me."

People who had "crossed over" often spoke to Marion. A gift? Yes. A burden? Even more so. When it happened in public, and she'd realize she'd answered aloud, she would turn as red as a home-grown tomato.

When Marion's apartment had been fumigated over two years ago, Amanda offered Marion a temporary stay in her funky, brown-shingled cottage at the back of a wildly overgrown lot. The arrangement became permanent.

Marion was straight; Amanda was a lesbian. They had become best friends and family. Each of their traits had rubbed off on the other. Marion's language had become more colorful, and Amanda sometimes remembered to think before she spoke.

"How was your run?" Marion asked.

"I did three blocks. Worked up quite an appetite. What's for lunch?"

"Kale salad with cottage cheese and tomato wedges," Marion replied

Amanda wrinkled her nose.

"Remember, we're trying to shed some of the weight we gained on that cruise last month."

"The cruise that almost killed me," Amanda said, stabbing a wedge of tomato.

"You were so obsessed with that woman who turned out to be a serial killer—you almost got yourself murdered," Marion corrected.

"Until *you* killed *her*," Amanda said.

"I thought we weren't going to discuss that anymore," Marion replied, forking a bite of cottage cheese into her mouth.

"Speaking of that 'thing we're not talking about anymore,' isn't this the week your probation officer visits?" Amanda artfully maneuvered her fork under a bit of cottage cheese to avoid the kale.

Marion had killed the psychopath who'd attempted to murder Amanda as she slept. A long list of extenuating circumstances helped Marion's prison sentence be reduced to one year's probation and community service.

"Yes," Marion said around a mouthful of kale. "Virginia should be here around three o'clock."

"Good thing you've managed to stay out of trouble and have nothing to report," Amanda said, grinning. She speared a tomato wedge. "And it's probably a good thing we've gone back into retirement from our sleuthing career."

Marion said nothing.

"I said—"

"I heard you." Marion sat back and lowered her eyes. Several moments passed. "I think we should go to that woman's funeral."

Amanda flinched. "What? Why?"

"I suspect more information will be revealed to help us—"

"Don't." Amanda cut her off mid-sentence.

"Don't what?"

"You were about to say, 'help us solve this mystery,' weren't you? What's the mystery? The coroner certified she died of a heart attack." Amanda sighed heavily. "Does the word *retirement* mean nothing to you?"

"But once she's in the ground, that will be that. Another old woman, easily disposed of."

"I'm exhausted," Amanda said. "We haven't had a moment to breathe since finishing the last case."

"We can't let her death become insignificant," Marion insisted. "There's something not right about her death. I can feel it in my bones."

Amanda slowly shook her head. "Okay, I surrender." She picked up their plates and carried them to the sink. "I'll do the dishes."

"Thanks. I'll run the vacuum before Virginia gets here."

———

When the doorbell chimed, Marion patted her hair, straightened her blouse, and opened the door.

"Virginia, come in," she said. She guided the woman into the living room.

Virginia Mahoney wore a dark blue pantsuit with a County Sheriff emblem on the jacket. Although short in stature, the power she projected made her seem larger than she was. Her hair, short gray in the front and tied into a ponytail in the back, made her look like she had a squirrel balanced on her head.

Virginia knew Marion socially. They'd worked together on the local library book drive for years and knew many of the same people.

"You know, I followed your case in the papers and attended the court hearings. I'm just so sorry all that happened to you and Amanda," Virginia said. "It feels uncomfortable, but I've got to ask you a bunch of questions."

"Perfectly alright," Marion assured her. "It's your job."

Virginia ascertained that Marion had not used illegal drugs nor alcohol and had not been fraternizing with felons. She reminded Marion not to travel out of state without permission and to appear in Court as required.

"Yes, yes, of course," Marion agreed.

"And then there's community service," Virginia said almost apologetically. "What would you say to spending an hour a week picking up litter at the local park, maybe help the landscape crew?"

"That would be just perfect," Marion said, smiling broadly. "I haven't been getting much fresh air or exercise lately."

They chatted briefly about friends in common and then Virginia left.

Amanda stuck her head into the living room. "How'd it go?"

"Being an ex-felon isn't as hard as I thought it would be," Marion replied.

———

The next morning, Marion clomped into the kitchen, plunked into the nearest chair, and kicked off her grungy work boots. "Scratch that wonderful-day-in-the-park-getting-fresh-air-and-exercise thing," she muttered. "That place is disgusting! And the people? Creepy."

Amanda turned off the flame under the teapot and gestured to Marion who nodded. Amanda poured two mugs of tea and brought them to the table. "Disgusting? Creepy? Our local park?"

"We have to wear thick gloves, so we don't get stabbed by dirty needles scattered about or bugs from the filthy discarded blankets and clothes. And these God-awful boots! Stomping around and navigating around the dog and people poop. I could go on—"

"People poop?" Amanda snickered. "Seems like a harsh punishment for saving my life." Amanda blew into her mug. "I figured there'd be moms and kids at the park."

"Oh, there were, over by the playground area. Although on the fringe, scruffy, filthy, red-eyed guys, hung around drinking from bottles hidden in paper bags. They shout at each other as if they're hard of hearing and call each other by names like Doc, Paco, and Jimmy the Jaw. It's horrifying."

"You work in teams for safety, don't you?" Amanda asked.

"Oh, yes. My teammate is Tilly, a two-hundred-pound ex-hooker working off a minor drug possession charge. She felt right at home."

Amanda tried to disguise her chuckle as a cough. "Good thing it's just once a week," she said and grinned behind her mug.

Chapter 3

One Month Earlier

A banging at the door interrupted Audrey Cuthbert's creativity. She sat at her dining room table, a rainbow of ink pads, paper, and ink stamps spread in front of her. Unaccustomed to company, she paused before answering the door.

Bang. Bang. Bang.

"Well, good heavens," she muttered. She tossed her trifocals on the table and stuck a few strands of errant white hair behind her ear. She scooted her chair back, stood, then noticed the increased *crack*, *snap*, and *pop* of her aging body as she walked down the hall. Opening the door as wide as the chain lock would allow, with beady black eyes, she regarded the man on the other side. His unkempt hair looked greasy, and he needed a good shave. He looked unhealthy with his sallow complexion and skeleton-like frame. Shabby clothes hung on him like wilted leaves on a dying weed.

"No solicitations," Audrey pointed at the mat in front of the door.

"Aunt Audrey, it's me, Toby." As if he had asthma, he wheezed when he spoke.

"Tobias?" She blinked her confusion.

Tobias must be in his thirties, she thought as she appraised him. Last she'd seen her nephew was at her brother's funeral. Twelve at that time, Tobias lived with his mother. Audrey had always wondered if the contentious divorce had played a part in her brother's heart attack.

With some reluctance, Audrey unlatched the chain and opened the door.

"Come in, Tobias. I wish I'd known you were coming. I could have prepared . . ." She looked past the front steps. The only car out front was her new Taurus. Toby carried a gym bag but nothing else.

"How did you get here? How long are you staying?" she asked as she shuffled him into the kitchen. He looked malnourished.

Audrey pointed him to a chair, and he sat.

"Things weren't working out so well in Florida." He hung his head and sighed. "Lost my job, then my apartment, then my girlfriend. Just the way it goes, I guess." He gave a listless shrug. "Figured I'd try the other coast for a while." He looked up at her with dull, dead-fish eyes. "I hitched," he said flatly.

Audrey grimaced despite herself. As repugnant as this young man was, he was the only child of her dead brother and had sought her out.

"I'll heat some stew." Turning away, she took a breath and collected herself.

From the refrigerator, she took out a plastic container of stew and a package of buns. She pulled a bowl and pan from the cupboard and a ladle and spoon from the drawer.

"You wouldn't happen to have a beer, would you?" Toby asked.

"Milk, orange juice, water," she said, her tone held a clear message of disapproval.

"Water's fine." He shrugged off his jacket and revealed a sleeveless T-shirt. Instead of sleeves, tattoos covered his arms; symbolic images in vivid colors ran together like patterned fabric. "I could use a bath. Got in late and spent the night in the park with some guys." He gestured with his head.

What would Jesus do? she wondered as she heated the stew and warmed the buns. Audrey was not a Christian, but she was out of her league here. "How long did you say you were staying?" she asked.

Toby shrugged. "Gotta get me a job then a place to live."

Audrey served the stew, broke off two buns, and put them in front of Toby.

"I don't have a car. That's gonna make it harder. I could use temporary crash pad until I get it together."

"Oh, dear," Audrey mumbled.

————

"I'm going to be at my art class until noon," Audrey said the next day over breakfast. "I prefer you leave, perhaps look for work or whatever one does, until I return. Is that agreeable?" She wrinkled her forehead, somewhat embarrassed at the harshness of her message—she didn't trust him alone in the house.

"Yeah. I've got people to see." Toby downed his orange juice and took his plate to the sink. "Thanks for breakfast." He ducked his head and turned away.

One point for manners, Audrey thought.

They left the house, and Audrey clicked the lock behind her. "Will you be home for lunch?"

"Probably not 'til dinner," he said and struck off down the sidewalk toward the park.

———

Lively chatter and friendly bickering filled the art room. Living alone with only the company of her thoughts, Audrey looked forward to the sense of community she found among her classmates.

"And this one," Harriet Borger held up a newly acquired stamp, "is a Zen fish. Quite artsy, don't you think?"

"Looks like something you'd see in a tattoo," Alberta said.

Audrey's ears perked up. *Tattoo? Maybe that could be an inroad to connecting with Tobias. Both tattoos and ink stamps were symbolic.* If she found a stamp that represented something personal and wore it on her body like a tattoo, perhaps the commonality with Tobias would open up. Maybe he'd lose some of that pitiful loser attitude he wore like his bad-fitting clothes.

She squeezed into the chair next to Harriett. "How would I go about finding a stamp personal to me? Something similar to tattoo art?"

"Flash," Harriett said.

Audrey scrunched her forehead.

"Tattoo art is called flash," Harriett clarified.

As if Harriett had been in a tattoo parlor lately. Audrey smirked. *Some people are just so full of themselves.*

"The last tattoo I got was a mermaid," Harriett added. She hiked up her pants leg to reveal a stunning sea creature on her ankle.

Audrey gasped.

"Got it after my niece drowned in a boating accident on the Bay," she said, dabbing her moist eyes with a tissue. "This one . . ." Harriett shoved her sleeve up. A dazzling scorpion was tattooed into her upper arm. ". . . Is for my astrological sign, Scorpio."

"Well, I'm impressed," Audrey said, regretting her earlier sarcasm. "Those are quite artistic."

Class began, and Audrey set her materials in front of her but got lost in thought as she searched for the perfect stamp.

Audrey's astrological sign was Taurus, the bull. She'd often been considered bull-headed by people who didn't know that she was usually right. True, she had stacks of papers on her desk and a pile of books in the corner of her bedroom, but she knew precisely where any needed paper or book was within those piles. There were virtues to being a Taurus.

Hmm. Maybe a *bull.* She'd go online this afternoon and see what she could find. Audrey smiled. A conversation with Tobias about their mutual interest could create the start of a bond. Perhaps then, in her gentle way, she'd tell him to get his life together.

Although Tobias didn't return that night, he had obviously been there during the day—a breach of their agreement. The guest bathroom toilet hadn't been flushed. *Dear God*! Filthy socks laid curled up in the corner like sewer vermin and grime trailed along the lip of the sink basin. She regretted having shown him where the spare key was hidden and vowed to move it.

She had, however, been successful at finding an adorable bull stamp and a pad of sparkly silver ink. She was so tickled and had it sent one-day shipping from Amazon Prime.

Chapter 4

Today, Amanda pulled her VW into a parking spot alongside the church and gave an exasperated *harrumph*. The gall! Someone had hogged two parking spaces for their new silver Taurus.

"Just rude," she muttered.

Marion checked her hair in the rearview mirror before she joined Amanda on the curb. "I haven't been in a church for decades," she said. "Feels a little strange."

Amanda gave a hearty nod. "A lotta strange," she replied.

The small chapel—Marion supposed they called it "intimate"—was a recent add-on to the larger sanctuary in the old stone Methodist church. Narrow floor-to-ceiling stained-glass windows muted the hazy sunlight and created a cozy, yet somber, ambiance for the handful of mourners gathered for Audrey's funeral.

Marion signed the guest book, accepted a remembrance card from the usher, and followed Amanda into a pew near the front.

A scruffy, middle-aged man in an ill-fitting jacket sat alone in the front row. His quick and jerky movements accompanied his glances from one side of the church to the other. Every few minutes, he checked his watch.

"Must be the nephew," Amanda whispered. "Looks like he's on something."

"Probably just nervous," Marion replied. She studied the face on the card and smiled. Audrey reminded her of her great-grandmother with white curly hair, bright beady eyes, and strong bone structure. She noted the date of birth, May 8, 1938. She sat back suddenly, her jaw went slack, and her eyes lost focus.

Alarmed, Amanda grabbed her arm. "Marion?" She shook her gently. "Marion!"

Marion blinked and eased her focus toward Amanda.

"Marion, are you having a stroke? Can you speak? Do you know your name? Try smiling." Amanda rattled off all the things she knew to check for a stroke before she remembered a similar event happened at an ice cream store the previous year. Marion was having some sort of psychic "episode."

Just as the minister spoke, Marion stammered.

"I . . . I . . ." Signaling she was okay, Marion fluttered her hand at Amanda.

The minister reviewed Audrey's life. In her earlier years, she'd worked as a switchboard operator. Then she became a mother and a homemaker and supported her husband and son. Both preceded her in death as did a younger brother.

She was briefly a member of the church's Senior Circle, had recently taken an interest in the arts, and took classes at the Senior Center.

There was no mention of a nephew.

When the minister asked if anyone wished to say a few words, Amanda and Marion looked toward the jerky man in front who tucked his chin and averted his eyes.

"I Come to The Garden Alone" played through the AV system, a prayer was said, and the service ended. Touched by the music and their thoughts about dying, both women dabbed their eyes with tissues. Amanda blew her nose loudly.

Having recovered her faculties, Marion excused herself and slipped into the side aisle in time to intercept the man she'd been watching.

"Excuse me," she said. "Are you Audrey's nephew from Florida?" She gave him her most heart-warming little-old-lady smile and offered her hand.

As if taken off guard, the man stiffened and looked trapped. He tentatively shook her hand. "Toby Grier," he muttered.

"Marion," she said, attempting to make eye contact. "I'm so sorry for your loss."

Toby's eyes darted to either side of her then away. "Excuse me. I have to go." He hurried out the exit.

Marion followed. She stopped just outside the door to see Toby climb into the silver Taurus, back out of the parking spot and beat a hasty retreat down the street. She stood with her head crooked to one side. "Thought so," she murmured.

Marion caught up with Amanda, who chatted with several elderly women in the social hall.

"This is my friend, Marion," Amanda said, introducing her to the small circle of women. "They're from Audrey's ink stamping class."

"My condolences," Marion said. "Such a sad way to meet people."

Alberta Johnson nodded. "I was just saying that Audrey was so tickled about getting her new stamp—the cutest little bull." She wiped a tear with the edge of her handkerchief.

When Amanda and Marion had settled into their car, Amanda said, "So, what was happening back there in the church? You were having some sort of 'episode,' weren't you? Scared me for a moment."

"Ah, yes," Marion said. She rolled down her window for some air. "I was looking at Audrey's picture on the remembrance card, and she whispered to me, 'Follow the bull. Don't let him get away.'" Marion shrugged her shoulders. "I have no idea what she means."

"The bull? Alberta mentioned a bull stamp. Could that have something to do with her death?" Amanda paused a moment then said, "I need paper. Let's go home and make a list about how the word 'bull' has shown up this week."

"As good a place to start as any," Marion said.

————

They sat at the kitchen table and attempted to list all things 'bull,' but Amanda's cat, Cali, made herself at home atop the paper. Marion gently lifted Cali to the floor and wiped cat hair from the table with a napkin. Not being a "cat person," she'd almost overcome her impatience with the inconvenience of living with one.

"Okay," Amanda said, rubbing her hands briskly together. "It all started at the fair."

"What did?"

"Clues. Things with 'bull' in them."

"But we didn't even know she was dead yet. It wasn't until after the fair that you saw her obituary."

"Marion, you sound like a normal person. You've said there is no 'time' in the spirit world. Right?"

Marion nodded.

"So," Amanda continued. "I'm thinking she was sending messages right after she died. It just took us a while to catch up."

"Do you know how weird this conversation would sound to anyone else?" Marion grinned. "Okay, go on."

"There was the mechanical bull that threw me to the ground."

"That's one."

"Two, there was the bulls-eye I hit and won a stuffed bull," Amanda said, her voice rising in excitement. "I guess that would be two and three."

"Four," Marion chimed in. "The bully I stopped from taking his brother's cotton candy. Okay, so I called that one wrong, but it still has 'bull' in it."

"And how about the '*bull*-own-y' sandwich?" Amanda caught her bottom lip between her teeth.

"That's not how it's pronounced . . ." Marion said. "Oh, whatever. Okay, number five, bull-own-y."

"Yes," Amanda said with a self-satisfied grin. She made a victory sign with her arms.

"Now what?"

"Hmm. Well, she'd just bought a bull stamp," Amanda said.

"Wait a minute." Marion retrieved the remembrance card. "Yes, this is it. Look at her birthdate." She handed the card to Amanda.

"May 8, 1938. Is the year significant?" Amanda asked.

"No, but her birth month, May, is. Her astrological sign would be Taurus, the bull. Hence, the stamp?"

"Whoa!" Amanda wiggled her fingers at the 'woo woo' of it all. She thought for a moment and then said, "And Taurus, the silver car! The one that the twitchy man drove. I wonder if it was Audrey's?"

They exchanged a charged look.

"It would be way too soon for her estate to be settled," Marion said. She sat back, tapped her fingers on the table, and willed the next piece of the puzzle to come to her.

"*Don't let him get away*. Isn't that what she whispered to you?" Amanda said. "What if the nephew killed the old lady and stole her car?"

"Possible, I suppose. But if he's the only heir, why wouldn't he wait for the inheritance?" Marion got up and paced the kitchen.

"I think we need to do a little background check on Toby Grier," Amanda said.

Chapter 5

Three Weeks Earlier

"Tobias, do you have a moment?" Audrey regarded her nephew who slumped at the kitchen table; an opened beer can set in front of him. His shoeless feet were clad in once-white socks, and his hair was slicked back without hair product.

Toby flipped the pages of *Cycle World*, a popular motorcycle enthusiast's magazine. After a bored-with-life sigh, he glanced at Audrey.

"I want to talk with you about your tattoos," her words oozed with eagerness.

Toby's eyes became guarded, and a scowl rearranged his face.

"They're quite interesting, and I wondered if you'd tell me what they're about."

As if he'd misheard her, Toby blinked and crocked his head.

"I do have an appreciation of flash." She tried out her new word and checked to see the effect it had on Tobias.

"It's similar to the ink stamping I do, though mine is much less sophisticated," she added.

Toby straightened up in his chair. "What do you want to know?"

Although his voice was tentative, his interest seemed piqued. *After all*, Audrey mused. *How many old women used the word "flash?"*

Audrey took a seat across from him, leaned forward, and pointed to his bicep. "That, for instance." She pointed to a motorcycle with wings. "What does it mean?"

Toby looked at his arm, his lips forming the semblance of a smile. "I call that Bat Outta Hell. It's how I feel when I'm full throttle on my bike. Well, when I had a bike, that is."

"I don't know if I've ever felt like that," Audrey admitted. "What's that one?" She pointed to his shoulder. "It looks sort of . . ." A rose color climbed her neck and overtook her face.

"Sexual?" Toby said. "It's a Scorpion, my Zodiac sign. The stinger is a penis. Has to do with prowess, power, and danger."

"Excuse me a moment," Audrey scooted her chair back. "There's something I want to show *you*."

When Audrey returned, she took the chair next to him and opened a spiral binder.

"I'm not brave enough to put these on my body, but I do like arranging the images create to a picture statement—like a collage," she said. "Like this rabbit in the cornfield." She pointed out the stamped repetition of cornstalks that looked like a small field. An ink-stamped rabbit looked lost in the maze.

"Sometimes, I feel like this when faced with new projects—especially those having to do with computers. I get lost and forget how to find my way out." She hadn't planned to reveal this much, but there it was. She looked over at Tobias.

"What's that one?" Toby chuckled at the image on the next page, a blue bull among a garden of flowers. "He looks a little out of place."

"That's my zodiac sign, Taurus, the bull. It's a part of my personality I'm not so thrilled with—you know, stubbornness. So, I try to compensate for my bullish nature by softening my presentation."

"The sweet-little-old-lady thing," Toby said. "Like *Steel Magnolias*? I saw that movie." He blushed slightly.

"Something like that," Audrey replied. That was as close to anything resembling a compliment she was likely to get from her nephew.

"You should try it on your wrist," he suggested.

"Oh, I don't think so," Audrey said, shaking her head. "My skin's too old and wrinkled to carry off a tattoo, even one from an ink pad."

Toby surprised her by reaching over, turning her palm face-up, and lightly tapping her wrist. "Right there," he said.

At that moment, his cell rang, and he left the room to answer it. Five minutes later, he was out the door.

Well, it's a start, Audrey thought.

———

Doc, Paco, and Jimmy the Jaw lurked deep in the shadows at the back of the park. Toby sauntered over as they passed a bottle of Wild Turkey around.

"Yo, Tobe," Paco called him over.

"S'happenin', man?" Toby accepted the bottle and took a long swig.

"What 'chu been up to?" Doc asked. "Hanging out in that fancy-ass house, stuffin' your face on free grub?"

"Gettin' any on the side?" Jimmy asked with a leer.

"Aw, man, that's my old aunt you're talking about. That's disgusting," Toby said. He shuffled about, spat on the ground, took a joint out of his jacket pocket, and lit it. After a deep hit, he passed it on.

"Primo, dude." Paco coughed his approval.

"So, my aunt decides we're gonna have some bonding time and asks about my tattoos, like what they mean and shit."

"Ha!" Doc slaps his leg. "You show her the pussy on your chest?"

Toby fixed him with a stare. "Then, she brings out this scrapbook thing. Starts showing me her ink stamp pictures, like it's as cool as my tats. She's got this bull she dipped in blue ink. I say she oughta stamp it on her arm, not on a piece of paper. She gets all freaked out." He snickered self-consciously, unsure of why he was telling them this.

"When we gonna get to hang out at your house? Startin' to get cold out here at night, ya know," Paco said.

"Yeah," Doc added. "We could come for dinner, share our tattoo stories with the old broad. She should probably meet the fine young fellas you're hanging out with, don't ya think?"

"Didn't you say you were her only relative?" Jimmy asked. "Like you get everything when she dies?"

"What's your point?" An uncomfortable feeling passed through Toby.

"Just sayin'. You owing the boss man down south a shitload of money. You fuckin' had to run for your life. I mean, she's old and all, anyway."

"Old folks have accidents all the time, man," Doc threw in. "I got a connection for a nerve agent—from a Nam vet—makes it look like a heart attack."

"Hey, back off," Toby said. He spun around and faced them. "No one's killin' off my aunt. Got that?"

"No offense, man. Just thinking out loud, ya know? House, car, bank account, major debt."

Chapter 6

Two Weeks Earlier

"I'm just going to run up and change clothes," Toby called over his shoulder. He stopped halfway up the stairs and added, "Don't touch anything. I'm not supposed to be in here during the day, and you're not allowed here at all." He shot Doc a warning look before darting up the remaining stairs.

"Pussy," Doc muttered. He roamed around the living room, checked out the kitchen, hovered over the table in the dining room where a variety of ink stamps and pads were neatly arranged.

Doc heard the shower running and glanced up the stairwell. Now was his chance. An idea had been rattling around in his mind like dice in a cup for a few days.

Doc opened up the silver ink pad and saturated it with the contents of a small vial hidden in his jacket pocket, then slid the inkpad back into its place. He ripped a page from one of the spiral binders, scribbled a quick note, and signed it *Tobias*. He placed the bull stamp on top of the note and moved it where it would be seen. Risky, he knew, but that's what gave him the dark thrill that ran like a shot of meth through his veins.

The shower was no longer running. Toby must be getting dressed.

Doc wandered back into the living room. Out of the curtained front window, he noticed a car pull into the driveway. *Shit!* Driven by instinct, he jumped into the cloak closet and buried back as far as he could. He hoped the old broad didn't need to hang up anything. He'd escape when she left the room. Toby, however, was on his own.

A key turned in the lock, and the front door swung open. Footsteps passed by the closet. Just then, a loud boom shook the house. For seconds, the walls vibrated, and a wave rippled the floor like an unsteady sea.

Earthquake! Doc realized as a hatbox tumbled from the shelf above and fell on his head.

————

Upstairs, Toby had heard the car drive up and the front door open.

Caught.

He could explain his way out of being home during the day if he had to, but what about Doc? Then an explosive sound caused him to jump. The rumbling house threw him off balance, and he fell onto the bed. Panicked, he tried to get his footing.

Audrey, having lived through many earthquakes, bolted for the sturdiest doorframe in the house. She clung to the frame as the house shook. Dishes crashed to the floor in the kitchen. The rumbling stopped in under a minute. She unclenched her hands from the doorframe and crept into the kitchen to assess the damage.

Using the lull, Doc jumped from the closet and bolted out the front door. Toby sneaked down the stairs, checked for clearance, then took off.

Audrey busied herself picking up shards of pottery plates and broken glassware from the floor. "A good four-point-seven," she ventured. Just enough to rattle the nerves but not do any significant damage.

Because of possible aftershocks, she secured remaining dishes and closed the cupboard doors. *That's the trade-off for living in California.*

She worked her way into the dining room. Everything seemed more or less in place. She picked up a couple of ink pads and stamps now on the floor and restacked several books that had tumbled from a chair in the corner. Glancing at the table, she noticed the note, picked it up, and stuck it in her pocket to read after she'd assessed the damage to the rest of the house.

The living room had survived. Audrey straightened the pictures on the wall and returned a toppled floor lamp to its proper place. From there, she moved to her bedroom.

She righted the framed picture of her husband and son that had fallen over on the dresser and moved shifted jewelry boxes away from the edge. No damage there. Tobias could check the upstairs when he came home that evening.

Audrey remembered the note in her pocket and pulled it out.

Aunt Audrey,

> *I like that we share an appreciation of art. Maybe I got that gene from you? I promise to try one of your stamps if you'll try some body art. Stamp the bull in your new silver ink and place it over your wrist, just where your pulse beats. It would mean a lot to me. See you later,*
> *Tobias*

He'd drawn a happy face after his name.

Audrey smiled. Somehow, she'd gotten through to her nephew. The idea of sitting down with Toby and creating an ink-stamp picture on paper tickled her as much as wearing a silver bull on her wrist. She crumpled the note and tossed it in the wastebasket.

Four o'clock. He'd be home in an hour. Audrey sat down at the dining room table, opened her silver ink pad, picked up her sweet bull stamp, and saturated it with the ink.

The veins on her left wrist made a loop just below the base of her palm, and the bull fit nicely into that little corral.

Audrey pressed the stamp to her skin. Was a relationship with her brother's only child possible after all? It would be nice to have an heir. She leaned back in her chair and admired the silver bull glistening on her wrist. *Taurus. Own your sign*, she thought.

The image wavered before her eyes. She blinked to clear her vision to no avail. Under her hairline, a fine line of sweat broke out and crept down the sides of her face to her neck.

She was too old to be having a hot flash. She'd been done with those a couple of decades ago.

Audrey's tongue felt thick, and her cheeks numb. She reached for her face, but her arms failed her and fell to her sides.

What was happening? Was she having a stroke?

Pain seized her chest. As she panted to get her breath, the room seemed to recede, and her vision went dark. She had a sensation of falling, falling, falling.

———

Two hours later, Toby came home. "Aunt Audrey, you okay?" he called as he stepped into the hallway. "I heard we had an earthquake. We don't have those in Florida." Finding the living room empty, he walked into the dining room.

There, on the floor, was his aunt, her skin ashen and waxy. Her opened eyes fixed on nothing.

Toby froze. He knew dead when he saw it. Plenty of folks OD'd.

I should call 911, he thought, trying to figure out the ramifications.

Toby backed out of the room, turned down the hallway, and ran out the door. By the time he reached the park, darkness had settled in. Shadowy figures moved about in the back fringe.

"Yo, Tobe," Paco's familiar greeting rang out as Toby approached.

"S'up, man?" Doc clapped him on the back and handed him a can of warm beer.

Already three sheets to the wind, Jimmy the Jaw snickered.

Toby guzzled the beer, wiped his mouth with the back of his sleeve, and said, "My aunt, man. I think she's dead."

"Old people die," Paco offered his form of consolation.

"But . . . but . . . ." Toby stammered. "She's the only person I had left. Now there's no one."

"Those tears in your eyes?" Paco stared at Toby. "Shit, man."

"You're welcome," Doc said. The light from a distant streetlamp showed the grin on his face. "I see financial freedom in your future."

"Did you . . .?" Toby was at a loss for words. "How . . .?" He turned and puked in the bushes.

"So, you go home, you find your poor, dear aunt dead of a heart attack, and you call 911," Doc advised. "They take her away. You tell them you've never dealt with anything like this before and ask for their help."

"Yeah, then tomorrow, we come over to console you—eat, shower, sleep in clean beds," Paco added.

"They'll help you make arrangements. I'd advise cremation. You'll get death certificates so you can close out her accounts, settle her bills, and all that," Doc said.

"Then you're set up with a house, a new car, all her money. Easy street, man."

Doc made a formal bow from the waist and added, "Again, you're welcome."

Unable to face what needed to be done, Toby spent the night in the park. The following morning, he crept into the house and darted up the stairs to his room. After rumpling the bedspread and sheet to look like he'd slept there, he skulked down the stairs.

At the entrance to the dining room, he stopped, covered his eyes like a child watching a horror movie, and peeked through his fingers. She hadn't moved. It was time. Toby dialed 911.

Chapter 7

Toby's aunt's body was at the funeral parlor where he'd been talked into having a "small, but tasteful" service at the nearby Old Cross Methodist Church. A burial followed in the attached cemetery.

Thumbing through papers in Audrey's desk, Toby found a document outlining her wishes upon her death. She'd left the disposal of her property to her sole heir.

He supposed a barrage of legal papers needed to be signed, but Doc was right. His financial future was assured. Whether he could afford to wait around was another question.

Today, he had to get through the funeral. He packed the few clothes he'd accumulated, anything of value from the house that would fit into her three suitcases, to her bank accounts—and a shoebox of cash stuffed in the back of her closet.

Along with the car, which he could sell once he returned to Florida, he should have enough to pay off his debt and remove the price tag from his head and the target off his back. He'd come back later and deal with the house.

Maybe Sonja would come back if I could promise her a house and a better life in California. He could see turning his life around or at least the possibility.

He hadn't gambled since he'd gotten to his aunt's. The wager about how much Jimmy the Jaw could drink in one sitting, well, that hardly counted. And his aunt hadn't missed the twenty-dollar bill he'd lifted from her purse; she'd have said something.

He threw the bags in the trunk and hopped into the Taurus. Shame to sell this car. It was the best ride he'd ever had. Eye on the goal, he reminded himself.

Toby pulled up at the side of the church and angled his way between two parking spaces. He couldn't afford any marks or scuffs on the Taurus.

Unsure whether he could sit through this service, Toby sat in a pew and fidgeted. The last funeral, his father's, had produced years of nightmares, where his father would sit up in his casket and yell at Toby for being such a loser. He tapped out a cigarette, smoked it in jerky puffs with the window rolled down, then threw the butt on the ground.

He popped an "upper," not only to get high, but to help him get through the ordeal. The stimulant jump-started his heart rate from normal to fast. A trace of sweat ran along his hairline.

"The fuck," he said.

For a moment, paranoia took over. His mouth was too dry, and his scalp itched. Had Doc slipped him a deadly pill? Maybe he planned to move into Audrey's house and take over his inheritance. He glanced in the rearview mirror. His pupils were pinpricks and his jaw muscles ached from his unconscious clenching and grinding of his teeth.

Toby opened the door and swung one leg out. So far, so good. The other leg followed, and he pushed himself to a standing position. A little shaky, but he could do this. *Screw Doc*, he thought.

An old woman stood at the entryway to the chapel and shoved a card with a picture of his aunt at him. The motion caught him by surprise, and he gasped. The woman crooked her head at him. "Memorial card," she said as if he were an idiot.

He averted his eyes, headed down the outside aisle, and settled in a pew near the exit. He wasn't going to look in the casket, that was for sure.

Chapter 8

A tap at the door caused Amanda to lean back in her computer chair. With a yawn, she stretched her arms back, cricked her neck from side to side, and rubbed her eyes.

"Anything on Toby?" Marion breezed into Amanda's bedroom and peered over her shoulder at the computer monitor on Amanda's desk.

"Amazing what you can find if you know where to look and whom to contact," Amanda said with a grin.

"Our lad was a high school drop-out with a spotty employment history in Florida. Worked at an auto parts store, a service station, a convenience store. Did a little time for some misdemeanors: petty theft, disturbing the peace, small-time drug possession, those sorts of things. Oh, and there's a paternity suit on file."

"Doesn't surprise me. He seemed a bit sketchy," Marion said.

"There's probably more illegal activity that didn't get reported. He's had multiple addresses around the southern part of the state. His last landlord reported him as a missing person after Toby skipped out on two-months' rent. Vanished. That must be when he headed out this way."

"Well, there's still nothing to connect him with the possible murder of his aunt." Marion sank into a rocker, her chin resting on her chest. With a hangdog look, she said, "Is that it, then? What's the next step?"

"We could go over to Audrey's house and check it out."

"Oh, no. I don't like the sound of this." Marion closed her eyes and shook her head. We'd be messing with a potential crime scene. I *am* an ex-felon, after all." She stretched the neck of her sweater and took a shaky breath.

"What do you think they did with the body?" Amanda said. "There was no graveside ceremony."

Marion's bottom lip quivered. "*The body*. This is a person we're talking about here. It makes me sad."

"I know it does, hon, but you're honoring her life by seeing this through. Audrey would have appreciated that." She reached out and squeezed Marion's hand.

———

They parked in the empty driveway of Audrey's house.

"Do you think the car is in the garage?" Marion asked.

"He probably took the car, her money, anything he could sell, and beat it out of town," Amanda replied. She handed Marion a clipboard.

"What's this for?"

"We'll look more official if we have a clipboard. Let's check the house."

No yellow tape cordoned off the premises. Newspapers had been flung to the porch and lay scattered around the front door. Junk mail and fliers clogged the mailbox.

They knocked on the door and waited.

From the side yard, a neighbor wearing a bathrobe and scuffs approached with a shuffling gait. Like a toddler just woken from a nap, the man's white hair lifted in haphazard spikes.

"She ain't home," he said. "Hasn't been here for days. Who are you, anyway?"

Marion introduced herself and Amanda. "We're 'following up' on Mrs. Cuthbert's death." She pointed to the clipboard and apologized for breaking the news to him that way. "Were you close as neighbors?"

"Naw," he said, with no apparent emotion. "She died in there? Do they have to disclose that when they sell the house?"

Marion and Amanda looked at each other. "I believe so," Amanda said. "Do you know if her nephew is staying here?"

"That scrawny kid and his homeless buddies? No. Haven't seen them for days either." He wheezed in asthmatic breaths. "There go the property values," he mumbled before he turned and walked away.

"Let's try the door," Amanda suggested.

"Surely, it will be locked," Marion said.

"Not if the kid was the last to leave. Who bothers to lock a door when you're on the run?" Amanda turned the knob, swung the door open, and made an "after you" gesture with her hand.

A shiver ran through Marion, and she hesitated. "Can we get arrested for this?"

"Probably. Oh, yeah, the ex-felon thing." Amanda stepped across the threshold.

Marion squared her shoulders, took a deep, resolute breath, and followed.

On any other occasion, Audrey's house would have seemed cozy and welcoming. The sun streaming through the windows held no hint of warmth as it fell onto the gently worn oriental carpet.

The unpretentious furniture looked lived in. On the wall, a small collection of modern prints hung in silver frames. Art tablets, a spiral binder, tins of ink pads, and a collection of ink stamps covered the oak dining room table.

In the kitchen, a handful of dirty dishes sat in the sink, and the odor of not-taken-out garbage lingered.

The collection of rubber stamps—flowers, animals, cornstalks, trees—were discolored from pressing into the ink and then onto paper. Marion thumbed through the little booklet and smiled at the image of a blue bull surrounded by flowers and trees.

"Ferdinand," she said. The bull on the paper was blue, but the ink on the stamp was silver. "Hmm."

In that instant, Marion jerked and whiplashed her neck. She shot an arm out and grabbed ahold of the back of a chair to steady herself. "Oh!" she cried out, a look of shock on her face. Her skin was pale, her eyes wide, and her mouth frozen in in an 'O.'.

"What's happening?" Amanda rushed to her side. "What do you need?"

Marion pointed to the chair.

Amanda helped her sit then ran into the kitchen, grabbed a glass, and filled it with water. "Here, this will help ground you."

Marion recovered enough to emit a sardonic chuckle. "I can't believe you said that. You sound just like me."

Amanda frowned. "What happened?" she asked again.

"I felt like I'd been run into by a large animal. Knocked the breath right out of me." She looked around the room.

"What were you doing just before that?"

Marion took a minute to think. "Well . . . I noticed the ink left on the bull stamp was silver. The only picture with a bull was blue. Then, *wham*."

"Run over by a bull, were you? That's one way to get your attention. I think Audrey just gave us another clue." As if suddenly chilled, Amanda rubbed her arms briskly. "I'll check out the bedroom." Amanda pushed the door open and grimaced. "I wasn't cut out for this," she said under her breath.

———

Nothing seemed disturbed in the bedroom. Bed was made, clothes hung neatly in the closet, books tidy on a shelf. The wastebasket contained nothing more than a crumpled piece of paper. Amanda unfolded the paper and read the note.

Once she was back downstairs, she said to Marion, "Better sit down." She reread the note aloud.

Marion gasped. "Is it time to call Madison?"

Marion referred to Detective Madison Bright, who had helped them capture the serial killer a few months earlier. Through the harrowing ordeal, they'd gotten on a first name basis. He probably still thought they were crazy old bats, but a new respect haloed his tone when they'd last spoken with him.

"Maybe we could tell him we suspect foul play in Audrey's death, but can't prove it yet. He could have the body held a while to buy us some time. Wouldn't want any evidence destroyed," Amanda said.

Chapter 9

"Madison, thank you for calling back," Marion put the detective on speaker phone allowing Amanda to hear the conversation.

Amanda mouthed, 'It's about time.'

"Sorry for the phone tag," Detective Bright said, "It's been crazy around here with that triple homicide."

"Yes, of course, that would take priority. And, as I said in my message, I think we have enough proof to substantiate a further check into the death of Audrey Cuthbert. It appears it wasn't a 'normal' heart attack, and that her nephew, who had much to gain by her death, was somehow involved."

Amanda gave her a thumbs up for her summary.

"You're basing this on—?"

"Uh oh, here it comes," Amanda whispered.

"Well," Marion hesitated. "A rather cryptic message from Audrey herself and a note left for her by her nephew, Toby."

"A message from Audrey? Please tell me you don't mean . . ."

"Yes, posthumously. She appeared and said, 'Follow the bull. Don't let him get away.'"

Marion and Amanda nodded to one another.

"The bull?" Detective Bright said. "Would you two consider coming down to the office? I *think* I'd like to hear the whole story."

Their last adventure of crime solving with Madison, based on Marion's psychic abilities, had been a goose chase but ended in the capture of a serial killer.

"Absolutely," Marion said. "In the meantime, could you have the coroner hold the body for evidence? I understand she's been moved to the hospital morgue awaiting some documentation."

"What sort of evidence are we looking for?"

"A tattoo of a bull on her wrist," Marion replied.

There was an audible sigh on the other end.

They arranged a meeting for the following afternoon.

"Well, we have the rest of the day. How should we use it?" Amanda asked as she clicked off her conversation with the detective.

"Don't know about you, but community service calls. I'm off to the park. Ugh," Marion added.

———

"Tilly," Marion said, sidling up to her cohort park cleaner-upper. "Do you know any of those shady characters over there well enough to speak to them?" She angled her chin toward the line of trees bordering the back of the park, sat her black plastic garbage bag down, and readjusted her gloves.

Tilly swung her bulk around. She craned her neck and stared in their direction.

"Could you maybe be a little less obvious?" Marion said. She didn't want to draw their attention unless it was necessary.

"I left my opera glasses back at the halfway house. You want me to see, or not?"

"No need to be surly," Marion replied. "I'm looking for someone who lived near here," she said, remembering Audrey's neighbor's comment about the homeless guys who hung out with her nephew.

"*You* know someone who'd be hanging with these guys?" Tilly said. Her voice registered disbelief. "Okay, yeah, I kinda know Jimmy the Jaw. We was in Juvie together, back when."

"Do you think maybe you could introduce me?"

"You lookin' for a date or something?" Tilly wiggled her eyebrows.

Marion shivered at the thought.

"Yo! Jimmy," Tilly hollered across the park. She grabbed Marion by the elbow and dragged her along toward the three derelicts. "This here woman wants to talk to you."

As they approached, Jimmy looked at them with unfocused eyes and belched.

"Jimmy, you remember me, right? Juvie?" Tilly said. She was rewarded with a "hic."

Paco stepped forward. "What you want?" He looked the two women up and down and stepped directly in front of Marion. His breath reeked.

Marion wrinkled her nose and stepped back. "I'm looking for a young man named Toby. I thought you might know him," Marion said.

Paco looked at the third man who had turned his back as the women approached. "Doc, you want to handle this?"

Doc turned slowly and regarded them with a suspicious squint. "Maybe. Why would you be looking for him, and what's in it for us?" He continued digging at his thumbnail with the tip of a sharp knife, ran his tongue along dry, cracked lips, and slid his gaze up her body.

"You do know him, then," Marion said. She took a ragged breath to steady herself. Surely, he wouldn't stab her right here in the park during the day.

Wondering how much she should share, she fabricated on the spot, "He stands to inherit a decent sum of money, but we can't find him."

"And you would know this how?" Doc regarded the garbage bag, boots, and gloves, his point clear.

"It's a long story," she hedged. "If we found him because of a lead you gave us, I imagine he'd be mighty grateful. Perhaps he'd want to reward you?" She knew her ruse was a long-shot.

"He blew off for Florida," Paco said, suddenly less hesitant to talk. "You find him; you tell him he owes us, big."

"Any idea where in Florida?" Marion said. She was met with a cold glare. "Well, thank you for your time."

"See ya' round," Tilly said as she and Marion picked up their garbage bags and headed toward the less unsavory part of the park.

"Whew, that was close," Marion said after they were out of earshot.

————

The next day, Marion and Amanda sat across from Madison Bright and told their story. He shook his head slowly.

"This note," he said, turning it over and rereading it. "You think that it indicates her nephew's intent to kill her? It seems more like a friendly, family bonding-thing."

"Except for her command to 'follow the bull,'" Amanda said.

"There's still the question about why the ink on the stamp was silver not blue," Marion added. "If she did take him up on it and stamped her wrist with silver ink and died afterward . . ." she took a deep breath and let it out. "Don't you think we should at least see if she has a bull on her wrist and maybe do a tox screen or something?"

"You've been watching *CSI* again, haven't you?" Madison chewed his bottom lip. "I suppose it's worth a shot," he said after a long pause. "I'll call the medical examiner."

"Maybe you should put out an APB on Toby in Florida?" Amanda added.

"You're pushing it," Madison said. He stood, indicating the interview was over.

———

Later, after a rerun of *Law and Order*, *SVU*, Amanda said, "I'm kind of glad Madison is on this case. Takes the weight off our shoulders."

"If he sees it all the way through," Marion countered. "Our evidence is circumstantial at best. Do you think he'll keep us in the loop?"

Amanda shrugged.

"Does the front door look like it's leaning a little to the left to you?" Amanda said, holding up her hands like a photographer framing a shot.

"You mean since the earthquake?" Marion squinted across the room. "Maybe. Let's check tomorrow. I'm ready to call it a night."

"Just what I need," Amanda groused. "Structural damage." She turned off the TV and headed to her room.

Hours later, Marion woke to a white-haired, beady-eyed old woman bending over her. She tried to scream, but no sound came out. Eyes wide, Marion stared at the woman.

"No, no, no. It's the doctor," the woman said before fading away into the ethers.

Marion bolted upright in her bed and turned on the bedside lamp. Her heart raced, and she gasped for air. The room was empty. "Calm, calm, slow deep breaths," she whispered. "It was just a visitation." She put on her robe and slippers, padded across the hall, and knocked on Amanda's door. "Amanda, are you awake?"

Marion heard a shifting about.

"Well, I am now. What do you want? It's two in the morning," Amanda grumbled.

Marion opened the bedroom door and tiptoed in.

"No need to tiptoe; I'm up." Amanda sat against the headboard and clicked on her bedside lamp. She scooted over, making room for Marion. "Nightmare?"

"No, we've made a terrible mistake. We're wrong. It was her doctor," Marion rambled. "There goes our credibility."

"I cannot talk about the case at two in the morning," Amanda said, scratching her head. "Go write it down, and we'll talk about it over breakfast." She reached over, turned off the lamp, scrunched down, and pulled the covers over her head.

Marion sat for a moment; her shoulders drooped in discouragement. When she headed to her bedroom, she slammed Amanda's door louder than necessary. It was moments like this that her gift felt more like a burden.

The next morning, they sat at the kitchen table eating chocolate chip waffles—Amanda's specialty—eggs, and sausage. Marion refilled their coffee cups.

"She said it was her doctor?" Amanda leaned back in her chair, a quizzical expression on her face. "Was she taking medication? How could she, or he, have killed her?"

"I know. It's a puzzle," Marion said. "I'm not looking forward to sharing this piece of information with Madison—"

"Because he'll think we're lunatics," Amanda finished Marion's sentence.

With a sigh, Marion glanced across the kitchen. The message light on the phone blinked. "Looks like we missed a call," she said, rising to check the message.

"This is Madison," a male voice announced on the message machine. "Good news. Texas Highway Patrol picked up our boy just outside of Huston on an auto theft charge. Guess he wasn't smart enough to stay off the main highways. Anyway, he should be back in California within the week. We'll take it from there." He cleared his throat. "Good work, getting the car make, model and license number. Gave us something, uh, *concrete* to work with."

"Concrete, indeed," Marion huffed. "Did that sound invalidating to you?"

"You mean like 'the dead woman said follow the bull' wasn't concrete enough?" Amanda said. She couldn't hide her grin.

Marion tossed her wadded-up napkin at Amanda.

"Wait until he hears the latest update." Amanda teased.

"Oh, dear," Marion said. "That means Toby is innocent but will wind up in jail as soon as he gets back. Lordy, what a mess."

Chapter 10

"This is Detective Madison Bright. How may I help you?" He heard someone cleared their throat on the other end of the line. Madison crocked his head. "Hello?"

"Oh, hello, Madison. This is Marion. I thought I might get your answering machine."

"Nope. You got the real thing," he said, unusually perky. "Saved me a call. Looks like Tobias will be back here and securely in a jail cell by tomorrow evening. Then the real work begins."

"Yes, ah . . . that's what I wanted to talk with you about." Marion's voice wavered. She hesitated.

"I don't have a good feeling about this," Madison said. "What is it?"

"Well, it seems that Toby is innocent—"

"What?" Madison interrupted.

"Um, apparently the doctor did it," Marion's words tumbled out.

"The doctor did what? And which doctor would this be? And why would you even think this? Madison's voice raised with each question. "And do I even want to know?" he said, more to himself.

"I know this is upsetting, but please give me a moment to explain." Marion paced the short distance the cord would allow

Amanda sat at the kitchen table nervously shredding her napkin. "Better tell him to sit down," she said. "You know he's jumped out of his chair by now."

Ignoring her, Marion plowed on. "Audrey came to me in my sleep last night, hovered right over me, and said, 'No, no, no. The doctor did it.'" She listened to the silence on the other end of the line. "I don't know who her doctor is, but I think she, or he, should be brought in for questioning, don't you?"

Madison made a guttural rumbling sound that Marion couldn't quite discern.

"Let me get this straight," Madison said, his voice tight. "We have a likely suspect we've extradited on a murder charge who we may have falsely arrested because some ghost told you her doctor killed her—in which case we have nothing, zero, zip?"

"Well, yes. That's about right." Marion felt her pulse pounding in her head. "There's no way we could have known this earlier."

"I need a moment," Madison said. He hung up abruptly.

Eight days later, Marion could no longer tolerate the strain of waiting and called Madison.

"Sorry to bother you," she said when he answered, "I just wondered if there is an update to the case." On the other end of the line, she heard a long exhale of breath— the kind one does when he's counted to ten to calm himself down. She grimaced as she waited.

"The only doctor Mrs. Cuthbert saw in the last year was a month ago for her flu shot. She takes no medication. Apparently, our victim was in perfect health," Madison said.

"Well, that's good at least, I mean for the doctor, and of course for Audrey if she hadn't been killed." Marion babbled on. She caught herself, took a breath and asked, "What about Toby?"

"We're holding him for questioning. It's possible he'll be charged with accessory to a crime, having to do with an acquaintance of his called Doc. The story is pretty convoluted, something about Doc being left alone downstairs the day Mrs. Cuthbert died."

"Doc from the park? He's a shady character if ever I saw one," Marion said.

"You *know* this Doc?" Madison said, his voice tight with exasperation. "You might have mentioned this earlier. Two o'clock tomorrow. Be at the station." Madison hung up.

———

"I hate that I'm beginning to feel comfortably familiar with this place," Amanda groused the next afternoon as they were led into a small interview room in the County jail and sat down.

The door opened, and Madison's imposing figure filled the doorway while the two women sat in plastic chairs. He stood for a moment, regarded each woman, shook his head, then took a seat behind his large desk.

"I have a theory," Marion offered. She squared her shoulders and lifted her chin.

"I can hardly wait to hear it," Madison said, straight-faced.

"Well, what if the note Amanda found—"

"While illegally entering Mrs. Cuthbert's home?" Madison inserted.

"There was no crime tape, and the door was unlocked," Amanda said in self-defense.

"Could the note had been left by someone else? Someone like perhaps that Doc person. He could have tampered with the ink, right?" Marion gave Madison a pointed look.

"And what would this Doc have to gain from Mrs. Cuthbert's death?" Madison shot a sharp glance back at Marion

"We haven't exactly figured that out," Amanda said. "It might have something to do with sharing the wealth. The woman dies. Toby gets the inheritance and maybe shares it with his new homeless buddies?"

"That seems to be the theory Toby is sporting at the moment," Madison said, tapping his fingers on the metal desktop. "The problem is, that crew of degenerates seems to have conveniently disappeared."

"Not convenient for Toby," Marion said. "You've dusted the note for prints, right?"

Madison rolled his eyes.

"Seems there's not enough to hold him on for murder," Amanda said.

"He stole the car and left the state," Madison added. "Innocent people don't run."

"Well, that's one way to look at it," Amanda said. "His aunt is dead; he's the sole heir. So, he took her car before it was officially released to him, but he would have gotten it eventually," she reasoned. "Perhaps he was going back where he came from." She flashed an optimistic grin.

"He may be guilty of no more than unwisely taking advantage of a bad situation," Marion said.

"You two make me weary," Madison muttered.

———

Later that afternoon, Marion and Amanda debriefed from their interview with Madison. They sat on the living room sofa with a pot of tea and a plate of cookies between them. Marion poured them each a cup.

"It did sound like we were defending Toby, didn't it?" Marion said. "That must have been confusing for Madison, especially since we were so sure of Toby's guilt."

"That's before we had more information," Amanda offered.

"Thank you for validating words from the dead as information. I appreciate that," Marion said. She reached over and patted Amanda's hand.

"I'm not sure Madison does," Amanda said as she bit into a Fig Newton. "I wonder if he ever mentions us to his colleagues?"

They chuckled at the absurdity.

"In the end, it's important that they don't unjustly hold an innocent man," Marion said. "I think Audrey would be satisfied with this outcome, even if we didn't find her killer. We're trying our best."

"I do wonder what will become of Toby," Amanda said.

"I think we've not heard the last from him," Marion replied.

Chapter 11

"It's been two weeks with no dead people vying for your attention. Do you suppose it's safe to retire—again?" Amanda flipped through a *People* magazine she'd picked up at the grocery.

"I'm not comfortable with that word, 'retire,'" Marion said. She lifted a potted plant from the bookcase and dusted underneath. "What will we do with ourselves?" She dropped her dust cloth and sat down on the edge of the sofa. "I almost forgot to tell you. I ran into Betty Biggs on the street the other day."

"Betty Biggs is homeless?" Amanda said, eyebrows raised.

"No, not that kind of 'on the street.' Just walking, you know."

"Isn't she a little old for that? Anyone pull over while you were talking?" Amanda snickered behind her magazine.

"Oh, stop it before I forget what I was going to say." Marion tossed a pillow at Amanda.

Amanda lowered her magazine. "I'm all ears."

"Betty is in a community choir. They sing at local events, old folks' homes, hospitals . . . you know. They meet in the basement of the Methodist church every Thursday night to practice."

"Your point?" Amanda squinted, awaiting the inevitable.

"She thought we might like to join." As if it were a done deal, Marion gave a quick nod.

Amanda raised both hands in objection. "I can't carry a tune in a sling."

"I don't think you have to sing all that well," Marion said. "It's more being involved in the community spirit. It would be a good way to meet some new people."

"Great. Tell me how it went," Amanda said. She picked up her magazine again.

"I can't go by myself," Marion said, sounding distressed. "Won't you come with me, at least for the first time?"

Amanda looked into Marion's puppy-dog eyes and felt all squishy inside. "Oh, alright. But I'm not joining."

The next evening Amanda pulled her VW into the parking lot of the Old Cross Methodist Church. She turned off the engine and gripped the steering wheel.

Marion reached for the door handle, then paused. "You are getting out, right?" she asked.

"This is the same place we were for the funeral last month," Amanda said.

Marion nodded her agreement. "Is that a problem?"

"I don't want anyone to think we're members or anything. I mean, we're parking in their lot all the time. Maybe we should have brought your car."

"This is only the second time we've parked here," Marion reminded her. "Is there something you're not telling me about you and church?"

Amanda shook her head, got out of the car, and led the way down the sidewalk. Printed on the poster attached to the main door were the words, Community Choir, with an arrow pointing to the side entrance. They followed the walkway around, opened the side door, and descended a flight of cement steps.

"I don't hear any singing," Amanda said.

"We're a little early. They probably haven't started yet."

At the bottom of the stairs, a middle-aged woman, dressed in a sleeveless T-shirt, painters' overalls and a baseball cap worn backward, slapped plaster on the wall and troweled it smooth.

"I'll ask this woman," Marion said. "She can probably tell us if we're in the right place."

As they approached, Marion said, "Hello, how are you?"

Without making eye contact, the woman said, "Bloated. Got the curse. How are you?" She continued to slap plaster onto the wall.

Marion's eyes widened, her mouth fell open, but no words came out.

Amanda choked back a chuckle behind her hand.

Recovering slightly, Marion said, "Lost, perhaps. We're looking for the Community Choir."

The woman pointed down the hall with her trowel, which dripped a blob of plaster near Marion's shoe.

As they worked their way down the dimly lit hallway, Marion whispered, "What on earth was that all about?"

"Someone once said, 'If you don't want to know the answer, don't ask the question,'" Amanda said. She held the door open and followed Marion into a large, homey group room where the overstuffed furniture had been pushed against the walls. A table with coffee, tea, and water sat in one corner and a baby grand piano in another. Folding chairs, arranged in a circle, occupied the center of the room. About twenty-people milled about and chatted amicably.

A tall Ichabod-Crane-faced man dressed in skinny jeans and a plaid flannel shirt moved into the circle. The people settled into the chairs.

Marion scanned the room but saw no sign of Betty. She smiled at the man next to her who introduced himself as Mike as they shook hands.

"That's Stony, our leader," Mike said, shifting his glance toward the front.

"John, since you're closest to the door, would you call down the hall and ask Chase to lock the side door," Stony said. He consulted his watch. "I think we're all here."

"Who is Chase?" Marion whispered to Mike.

"You probably passed her by the stairs. General all-around handywoman who works for the church."

"Oh, my, yes we did meet—sort of." Marion gave an involuntary shudder.

"Hah!" Mike chuckled. "She's a piece of work, alright, but she can fix *any*thing."

Marion glanced at Amanda, who sat slumped in her chair with lips pressed tightly together. "You're such a good sport," she whispered to Amanda and patted her leg.

"Harrumph,"

The group spent the next ten minutes on introductions since each week brought new faces. A nice blend of men and women of various ages and ethnicities formed the community of singers.

"I see two new faces tonight," Stony said. He beamed at Amanda and Marion.

Marion stood and introduced herself. "Betty spoke highly of your group."

Amanda stood next and said, "I'm Amanda. I don't sing." Smiles and nods of appreciation circled the room.

"Many of us have been told we can't sing," Stony said. "We're here to break that myth. Janet, will you pass out the music please?"

"Uh, oh," Amanda whispered, "I don't read music either. Maybe I'll wait for you outside."

Before Marion could protest, Amanda slipped out of her chair, hurried through the room, and out the door.

Marion sighed.

———

Chase, the handywoman, sat on an overturned crate at the end of the hallway, apparently watching the plaster dry.

"Hey," Amanda said.

"Hey, yourself," Chase replied. "Pull up a crate and sit a spell."

Amanda did just that. "Thanks," she said, thinking, *this could be interesting.*

"I didn't take you for one of those choir-types when you came in." Chase gave Amanda the once-over.

"Didn't think you noticed me," Amanda said. "You were pretty focused on your work there." She pointed toward the damp plaster.

"People don't think I notice much," Chase said, staring at a spot on the floor. "I don't miss a thing."

Amanda chuckled. *Yes, indeed, this was an interesting woman.*

"I have Asperger's," Chase said. "Doesn't bother me. I hear it bothers some people. It bother you?" She glanced at Amanda then turned her head away.

"Not at all," Amanda said. "I'm pretty socially inept, myself."

"I figured. But I can fix things," Chase stated.

Amanda thought of the doorway frame that seemed atilt after the earthquake. Used to doing minor repairs and maintenance herself, she was wise enough to know that structural damage was out of her league.

"You do carpentry?" she asked Chase. "Shoring up walls and stuff?"

"Sure."

"Do you work outside the church? Like repairs and such?"

"Yeah."

"Do you have a card or something?" Amanda asked.

"Nope."

"A phone number?"

"Yeah."

"Could I have it? I'd like you to take a look at my doorway, see if maybe you could fix it."

Chase robotically recited her phone number.

"Wait, wait." Amanda got out her cell and clicked open her contacts. "Okay, one more time."

They sat a few more minutes, then Amanda said, "You think you could let me out? I'll wait in the car for my friend."

"Sure," Chase said. She followed Amanda up the steps. "You got drivers' heel. Heel's worn down." At the top of the steps, she unlocked the door then retreated to the basement.

Amanda climbed into the driver seat and sat grinning. She looked at the back of her right shoe. *By God, I do have drivers' heel*. Something about Chase endeared Amanda. She wanted to know more.

A half-hour later, Marion fastened herself into the passenger seat. "I wish you'd stayed just a little longer," Marion complained. "The music sheets were just lyrics. You would have known some of the songs. What did you do with yourself while you waited?"

"Found someone to work on the house," Amanda said.

"What? How? Where?"

"Chase. Turns out she's for hire," Amanda offered.

Marion slapped a hand over her heart. "You're kidding, right? That woman didn't seem of sound mind."

"She's a little odd," Amanda agreed, "but the church hired her. I'm willing to take a chance. There's something likable about her."

Marion shrugged.

Chapter 12

Saturday morning, a loud knock on the door shattered the silence. Marion, still in her robe and slippers, peeked out the window, saw Chase, and gasped. She opened the door and glanced at the clock. 7 a.m.

"Chase, come in. You're awfully early."

"Amanda said to come in the morning." Chase stood just inside the doorway.

"Well, come have a seat. She's in the shower but should be out in a moment. I'm Marion." She led Chase into the living room and pointed to the sofa. "Could I get you a cup of coffee?"

"No." Chase sat on the couch.

Marion took a side chair.

"Chase . . . that's an interesting name. Is that your birth name?"

"Elinore," Chase replied.

"Hmm," Marion smiled. "How did you come by the nickname Chase?"

"Used to run away from the commune. They'd chase me then drag me back. Guess that's where it came from."

"I see." Marion nodded. *This is one odd woman*, she thought as she sat in awkward silence.

"Well, good morning." Amanda walked into the living room. She rubbed her hands together, took a deep breath, and threw back her shoulders.

"Oh, thank goodness," Marion muttered to herself as she bustled off.

"What?" Amanda asked.

Marion shrugged and disappeared into the kitchen. Seconds later, she returned.

Chase and Amanda huddled as they peered at the angle of the doorway. Chase held a level, and Amanda squinted.

A ripple passed through Marion as the adage, "two peas in a pod," popped into mind. "Odd," she mumbled.

Within the hour, a confluence of noise surrounded the house—the ripping when they pulled off the siding, the buzzing as the saw chewed wood, and the nonstop hammering of the beams.

———

Marion spent the day shopping. When she returned later in the afternoon, Chase's pickup truck was gone.

Inside, Amanda sprawled on the sofa, her feet resting on the travel trunk they used as a coffee table. McDonald's wrappers and empty soda cups littered the top.

"What's this?" Marion said, her voice tight with judgment. She pointed at the mess. "You don't eat junk food."

Amanda grinned. "Chase got hungry. Thought I'd keep her company." She sat up to make room for Marion.

"That young woman is definitely odd," Marion said as she settled on the sofa. "She grew up on a commune, you know."

"I didn't know that," Amanda said. "I spent time at a commune. That doesn't make us peculiar."

Marion raised a skeptical eyebrow.

"Necessarily," Amanda amended.

"Anyway," Amanda continued, "Chase has Asperger's. That's why she's a little strange."

"Well, you think you know someone," Marion said, referring to Amanda. She kicked her shoes off, put her feet up on the sofa, and hugged her knees. "When did you live on a commune?"

"Remember, I told you when I was 17, I ran away from home and married a fool?"

"Oh, yes, the charismatic fool. You said he could talk you into anything."

"We moved to a commune in the Blue Ridge Mountain area for about a year."

"His idea?" Amanda nodded. "Why did you leave?"

Amanda seemed to sink into herself. Her eyes brimmed with tears. She dropped her head with a heavy sigh. "This is something I rarely talk about."

"I can see that," Marion said, her voice soft. "Sometimes, it helps to get things off your chest."

Amanda sat with that for a moment.

"I was pregnant. My boy-child husband wasn't into the family thing. He left." Amanda sniffed.

Marion handed her a box of tissues.

"My baby was stillborn. The midwife whisked her away before I could even see her. No reason to stay after that. As soon as I could move around, I packed my bag and ran away. I got pretty sick." Unguarded tears rolled down Amanda's cheeks.

"Oh, my God, I had no idea. I'm so sorry." Marion rested her hand on Amanda's leg.

Amanda took a deep breath. "Wound up at a youth hostel. People who ran it seemed kind. They took me in, nursed me back to health." Her eyes held a faraway look.

"I trusted them, felt safe. Then, they told me they were Baptists. I had to convert, they'd said, or my soul would be eternally damned to Hell. 'You'll never see your baby in heaven,' they threatened. I felt wounded and confused and finally ran away when I could separate my beliefs from theirs. I escaped with my soul intact and left the Ozarks for good." She smiled.

Marion sat speechless; her lips pressed tightly together. After a moment, she said, "Is that why you have an aversion to church?"

Amanda nodded.

"And probably why you have a soft spot in your heart for people who've had hard lives. You can 'relate,' as the kids say."

———

That night, Marion had a dream. A blueish-gray baby, eyes stuck shut, no life force in its tiny body suddenly turned pink and squalled. The cries woke Marion, who bolted upright in bed. The wailing had stopped. Catching her breath, Marion laid down, and after restlessness left her tossing and turning, she finally forced herself to stare at the ceiling until she willed herself back to sleep.

Chapter 13

The following evening, Amanda helped Chase gather her tools and put them into her truck.

"Chase, why don't you stay for dinner," Marion said as she approached them. "Nothing fancy, just spaghetti and meatballs, but we'd love to have you." She sent Amanda a *wouldn't-we* look with a nod.

"That's a great idea," Amanda said. "We both appreciate how hard you've worked." She looked back at her no-longer-leaning front entrance and grinned.

"Um," Chase said.

"Good," Amanda replied, patting Chase on the shoulder. "Let's go wash up."

———

Back in the kitchen, Marion gave the spaghetti sauce a final stir and turned off the burner. She cocked her head.

"Did you hear that?" Marion looked at the table where Amanda and Chase sat.

"I didn't hear anything," Amanda said.

"It sounded like a baby crying," Marion peered out the kitchen window.

"Might have been a peacock," Chase said. "Sometimes they sound like hollering babies."

"A *peacock*?" Marion raised her eyebrows. "Maybe we have new neighbors." She brought the sauce to the table.

Amanda started the rotation of dishes and passed the salad bowl to Chase who tilted the bowl and flicked salad onto her plate with her forefinger.

Marion's forehead wrinkled. "Why don't I just dish out the pasta," she offered. "The bowl is too heavy to pass around." She stood and forked out a serving for Amanda, Chase, and herself.

"I don't think you've ever dished out my pasta before," Amanda said, shooting Marion a curious look.

"You're welcome," Marion replied. "Sauce?"

When all serving disasters had been avoided, Marion sat back down.

"So, Chase, you mentioned you'd grown up on a commune," Marion said. "What part of the country was that?"

"Ozarks." Chase used her finger to twirl the loose ends of spaghetti around her fork. In deep concentration,

Chase held her slightly protruded tongue between her lips.

"Well, that's an interesting coincidence. Amanda spent some time in a commune in the Blue Ridge Mountain area."

"That's right," Amanda said as she broke off a piece of garlic bread. "I was just a kid."

"Are your parents still down south?" Marion glanced at Chase.

"Never had any parents," Chase said, around a mouthful of salad.

"That's tough—growing up without parents. What happened to them?" Marion continued.

"They left," Chase stuffed more spaghetti in her mouth. "The midwife raised me and the rest of the commune helped. I didn't stick around long."

"How old were you when you left?" Marion asked. "Striking out on your own must have been difficult."

"Don't know how old I was. Don't have a birth certificate. I did okay." Chase met Marion's eyes with a look that said Marion's game of twenty questions was over.

"More meatballs?" Amanda offered.

Chase accepted the plate and plucked up two more meatballs.

"Like the daughter I never had," Amanda murmured with a chuckle.

———

A knock at the front door caused all three women to crane their necks toward the living room.

"I'll get that," Amanda said.

On the front stoop stood a tidy, well-dressed, middle-aged man with a tentative smile. He could have been selling Fuller Brush, or vacuums, or Bibles, but there was no accompanying paraphernalia. He looked vaguely familiar, but Amanda couldn't place him.

"Hi. Is Mrs. Knox in?"

"May I tell her who's calling on her?"

"Toby."

"*Toby*? Mrs. Cuthbert's nephew, Toby?" Amanda said, taken aback.

"Uh, yes, ma'am."

"I'm sorry, I didn't recognize you. You're all . . ." She caught her thought before it fell out of her mouth. "Yes, of course, come in." Amanda called into the kitchen, "Marion, it's Toby."

She turned back to Toby and said, "We're having dinner, come join us. There's plenty."

Before he could protest or accept, Amanda took him by the elbow and wheeled him toward the kitchen.

Marion stood by her chair and gawked at him for a moment.

"Sorry to interrupt," he said. "Detective Bright said it would be okay if I came by to say thank you for clearing my name and all."

"You're welcome. I worried you'd be furious that I got you arrested in the first place," Marion said.

"I was. Then I heard about Doc's note. If I'd been you, I'd have made the same assumption."

Marion's eyes widened in surprise. This wasn't the young man she remembered from the funeral. In a short time, he'd seemed to have matured.

"Sit down, Toby. I'll get you a plate," Marion said, regaining composure. "Oh, and this is Chase, a friend of ours."

Chase stared at her empty plate.

"Hey," Toby said as he sat down.

"Hey," Chase responded, not looking up.

When Toby's plate was loaded and Chase's refilled, both Amanda and Marion, in their excitement, began a barrage of questions to fill in the blanks of their stymied case.

Between bites of food, Toby said, "After getting out of jail, I went back to Florida to pay off some gambling debts and finish up some personal business. Then I came back and moved into my aunt's house to settle her estate—her home, car, and her possessions. It was all pretty overwhelming.

"Meanwhile, Detective Bright pursued Doc and his cohorts, but the trail ran dry. It looked as though Doc had gotten away with murder.

"To be fair," Toby said, "I understand why he did it. Doc thought he was doing me a favor—making my life easier."

"Toby, it was murder! He killed your aunt," Marion said with exasperation.

"I'm sure he'd planned to cash in on that 'favor,'" Amanda added.

"Honor among thieves," Chase, for the first time, made eye contact with Toby. "I get it."

Toby smiled. "So, Chase, how do you know these two women?"

"They came to my work to sing," she said.

Toby, looking confused, glanced at Marion.

"We'll explain over coffee and dessert. Let's move into the living room," Marion suggested.

Chapter 14

For the next several nights, the squalls of an infant jolted Marion awake in the early hours of the morning.

"Just pick the child up already," she mumbled into the night. What neighbor was neglecting their wailing newborn? Was there a city ordinance against babies screaming at unreasonable hours? After all, there are rules in place for barking dogs or motorcycles revving their engines. Why not hollering babies?

"I'm turning into one of those crotchety, short-tempered old women," she said to Amanda over breakfast.

"Lack of sleep will do that to you," Amanda replied. "I sleep like a rock. The only baby that's cried loud in this neighborhood is in high school now." She poured them each a cup of coffee.

"Thank you." Marion passed the muffins. "Do we have anything planned today?"

"You have choir later. I thought I'd drive you there. See if Chase is around. I sort of miss her."

"I've never known anyone on the 'spectrum' before," Marion admitted. "She's rather interesting in an odd sort of way. So . . . unrefined, raw, unfiltered."

Amanda chuckled. "That's pretty much what you thought of me the first time we met."

"Oh, my." Marion blushed as she recalled their first meeting at a greasy-spoon. Amanda's gray hair, striped with pink and purple, had caught her eye. Amanda's long-sleeved T-shirt went to her thighs, and white leggings continued to her boots. Her multiple piercings and the snake tattoo on her neck shouted for attention. She ate with unrestrained gusto and belched loudly after their meal. "And, look where we are today." She smiled warmly.

———

That evening Amanda followed Marion down the church basement steps. Marion went directly to the choir room, and Amanda strolled to the basement to search for Chase.

She snooped around, poked her head into various rooms. With no sight of Chase, Amanda headed back up the steps. Just outside the entrance she heard a clip, clip and followed the noise around the corner of the church.

Chase sat next to an overgrown bush and snipped branches to form a rounded shrub.

"Nice work," she called to Chase. "I had hoped to find you here."

"Yup, this is where I am," Chase replied.

With some effort, Amanda squatted next to her. "I've missed seeing you. How have you been?"

"Can't seem to have an or gasm." She split the word into two. "Toby said women can have or gasms. I want one."

"Whoa!" Stunned, Amanda toppled over onto her ample fanny. "That's a lot of information to take in. I think it's time for another get-together. Are you free for brunch tomorrow, say eleven o'clock? In the morning, that is," she added, in case brunch wasn't a term Chase was familiar with.

"Sure."

"Okay then," she said, hauling herself upright with some effort. "I'm going to go back to the car to read until Marion's done. See you tomorrow."

"Sure."

———

"You're not going to believe this," Amanda said when Marion opened the car door and slid in. "I think Chase and Toby are having sex."

Marion's hand flew to her mouth. "Well, that certainly tops my news," she said.

"Which is?"

"We're having our first performance of the season at Shady Lane Rest Home this weekend. Isn't that exciting?" Her eyes lit up, and she grinned happily.

"That is exciting," Amanda said because she knew that was what was expected. Truthfully, the thought creeped her out. Nursing homes reminded her of their terror during their hunt for a serial killer who'd abducted and killed a resident about a year ago. She still had occasional nightmares.

"But, what's this about Chase, Toby, and sex?" Marion leaned forward. "I wouldn't imagine Chase knows a lot about that sort of thing."

"Right. That's why I invited her for brunch tomorrow. We should stop by the store and pick up some bacon, eggs, and maybe a half-dozen donuts," Amanda said as she backed out of the parking space.

Marion giggled. "I can't believe we're going to talk to her about sex."

"Why?" Amanda glanced at her. "We've both had it, at least."

"I suppose it's somewhere in my long-term memory bank," Marion said with a shrug.

———————

The next morning over brunch, Amanda said, "I've thought about what you said last night about orgasms, which is one word, orgasm." She cleared her throat and glanced at Chase, who dipped her donut into her coffee cup. That visual, plus the smell of bacon, distracted Amanda who'd limited herself to one donut and two pieces of bacon.

"Uh, huh," Chase said, after slurping her donut.

"Well, given you grew up on a commune, sort of without parenting, we were wondering what you knew about sex." Amanda flushed and fidgeted. This conversation was harder than she'd anticipated. She grabbed another donut.

"If you're having sex, we just want to make sure you are safe, dear," Marion added.

"Animals do it," Chase said, taking a swig of coffee. "People on the commune did sex. It makes babies sometimes. What does that have to do with or-ga-sm," she stretched the syllables into three as she tried out the new word.

"Yes, well." Amanda cleared her throat again. "Let's start with the basics. Sex can be between a man and a woman, where the man puts his penis in the woman's vagina." She glanced at Chase to see if she followed.

"You mean their hidey-hole." Chase nodded her understanding.

"That's how babies are made unless you're using birth control," Marion jumped in. "If you're having that sort of sex, we need to get you to a doctor and find the best kind of birth control for you. Unless," Marion shook her head vigorously, "you want to have a child."

"Geez, pass the bacon." Amanda took a slice and continued where Marion left off. "Sex can also be between two women, or two men, or a man and a woman without the penis-in-the-vagina thing, or even with yourself." She stopped, took a deep breath, and began again. "Sex can be for pleasure."

Chase raised her eyebrows.

"That's the orgasm-thing Toby told you about. Men and women experience it differently. A woman can give herself an orgasm by rubbing her clitoris, or a man can rub his penis . . ."

"Or they can do that to each other, just for pleasure," Marion added. "An orgasm is like an intense explosion of energy, centered right in your private area.

"The hidey-hole, I mean vagina, is where babies come out. But I don't know what a clitoris is." She looked at Marion.

"Oh, dear. Um, let me get a piece of paper and a pencil. I'll be right back." Marion stood up from the table and headed for pencil and paper.

"I know about vaginas because I helped Willow birth a baby on the commune once."

Amanda blanched, sat back suddenly, and dropped her donut to her plate.

"Did you say Willow was the midwife who raised you?" Emotion tightened Amanda's voice.

"Willow Chastain," Chase said as Marion rejoined them at the table.

"Oh, maybe that's why you're called Chase—a nickname for Chastain." Marion smiled and glanced at Amanda. "Amanda, are you okay?" She reached over, took Amanda's hand, and squeezed it.

"Willow was my midwife. She took my dead baby away. It has to be the same commune." She glanced at Marion with pleading eyes.

Marion gasped. "I didn't tell you about a vision I had right after you told me about your stillborn daughter." She noticed Amanda tremble.

"Chase, could you get the afghan from the couch in the living room, please? I think Amanda is going into shock."

"What about orgasms?" Chase asked.

"We'll get back to that later, I promise."

They wrapped the blanket around Amanda's shoulders and tucked it in. Tears brimmed on the edge of her eyes, and her lip quivered.

Marion scooted her chair close to Amanda. In a calm and lowered voice, she said, "The vision was of a newborn, bluish-gray, its eyes closed tightly, without life energy.

"I thought it was just the soul of the baby you lost, checking in, visually," she continued. "But then, the baby opened its eyes, took a breath, and cried. The color came into its sweet little body."

She checked Amanda, who stared at her wide-eyed, her expression unreadable.

"You know that infant I've heard at night, ever since we met Chase?"

Amanda nodded.

"I think that was your baby in search of its mother," Marion said. "I think she survived, Amanda. I don't know why Willow took her from you, but I don't think I'll hear her cry anymore now."

Marion glanced at Chase whose furrowed brows matched Amanda's.

"Are you saying . . . ?" Amanda's voice was hoarse. She stared hard at Marion and then at Chase.

Marion nodded, tears forming in her eyes.

With unguarded crying, Amanda reached over and took Chase's hand. "I think you're my daughter." Her voice choked with emotion.

"Okay," Chase said. "Can we talk about my clitoris now?"

The tension of the moment broke, and both Amanda and Marion howled with laughter, their tears a mixture of joy and shock at the new revelation.

"There aren't any legal papers or documents from back then," Amanda said, suddenly sober. "How will I know for sure?"

"They have paternity tests," Marion said. "Surely they have maternity tests as well. We'll do the research."

In their excitement, they'd forgotten that Chase might be clueless about the discovery and the implications it might have for her life. In her Asperger's fashion, she'd merely taken in the information on a concrete level.

"Chase, before we return to your clitoris, there's something we want you to understand," Marion said.

"When I was seventeen," Amanda said, "I lived in a commune. I think it was the same commune where you grew up. I had a baby . . .

"I was told by the midwife, Willow, that the baby girl was born dead. I never even got to hold her—they took her from me. If she had lived, she'd be in her mid-forties now, about your age. Are you with me?" She looked at Chase who appeared to pay studious attention.

"I was so broken-hearted; I ran away from the commune and never went back. Chase, I think that baby lived, and you are her. Willow's child was a hellion, and she decided to raise you as her own as well. She probably wanted another chance."

"That explains it, but it doesn't excuse it," Marion said. She looked at Amanda. "The amount of pain you must have endured." She shook her head. "All these many years later, you've found your daughter."

They both turned toward Chase, whose face showed no comprehension of the magnitude of this information.

"Chase, Amanda is your mother . . . or at least we think she is. We'll know soon."

"Okay," Chase said with the tiniest of smiles.

"And as your mother, I need to talk to you about sex, among a zillion other things," Amanda beamed. "My girl," she said with a heart full to bursting.

"This calls for another pot of coffee," Marion said.

"And a couple more donuts," Amanda added. Her mind spun with details. Did Chase have medical insurance? A decent place to live? I have an heir! What a concept.

The hours flew by as they shared history, talked about sex and bodies, and what it meant to build a family. Amanda and Marion secured a promise from Chase that Friday nights, now to include Toby, were to be family dinner nights.

After Chase returned to her groundskeeper cottage at the church, the women sat, splayed, and spent on the sofa. Amanda yawned loudly.

"Well, we solved something we didn't even know was a mystery," Marion said.

"Thanks to your gifts," Amanda said.

"I'm sorry I didn't tell you sooner about that vision of the baby alive and well. I was just so exhausted, I fell back asleep, and then it slipped my mind."

"I don't know if we would have put the pieces together any sooner if you had," Amanda admitted. "I'm still having a hard time wrapping my head around all this."

Chapter 15

"No, no. Not again. This is just not acceptable. I thought we were through. What more do you want from me?"

Amanda quietly opened Marion's bedroom door and stuck her head in. Marion paced as she ranted at some unseen being.

"I'm tired. I need my sleep. Please, leave me alone," Marion pleaded.

Amanda cleared her throat. "Um, Marion? You awake?" Marion was known to talk and walk in her sleep. "Who are you talking to?"

It was just after midnight, and the streetlamp cast a diffused light into the bedroom. Marion stopped in her tracks and looked at Amanda.

"What are you doing here?" she asked.

"You were ranting. I wanted to make sure you were okay. Was someone here?" She looked around the empty room.

"They're ganging up on me. A whole nursery full of crying babies. I can't stand it." She walked over to

Amanda and grabbed her by the arm. "Make them stop," she said, her voice filled with desperation.

"Okay, okay," Amanda said, trying to soothe her frantic friend. "This is another vision, right? With a message we've got to figure out, right?"

Marion nodded.

"So, once we know why, they'll stop crying . . . Probably," Amanda added. "Do you think this can wait until morning?"

Marion shook her head.

With a heavy sigh, Amanda turned on the overhead light. "Find some paper and a pen," she said.

Obediently, Marion located a small notebook and pen, crawled back in bed, and scooted over to make room for Amanda. With pillows plumped and covers up to their armpits, they set about with their technique—listing things they think and things they know.

"I know we're not done with the baby thing, or they wouldn't continue to cry," Marion said.

"I think the issue must be bigger than just me and Chase," Amanda added to the list.

They sat, stymied. "But, wait . . ." She turned her head toward Marion. "They can't all be dead babies. How is it they found you?"

"I wish I had an answer. Psychic gifts come in all forms, I guess."

"Okay, I'm going to throw out a what-if," Amanda said. "What if midwife Willow ran some sort of underground, black-market baby mill, or secret adoption service?"

"We'd need to know if there is a higher number of births on the commune without a corresponding number of residents, right?" Marion scrunched her brow. "Do you think they're impregnating the women and selling their babies? Like white slavery?" She shuddered. "That would be horrific."

"And the nursery full of crying babies wants us to pursue this? That's why they're not letting you sleep?" Amanda wiggled around to a more comfortable position. "There could be children, teenagers, adults by now if she began doing this after I left."

"We may have to make a trip to the Ozarks and work our way into the commune, interview the women who live on the land," Marion said. "Oh, I'm not looking forward to this at all."

"Let's not get ahead of ourselves. We can check with Chase. See what she remembers of her childhood there. She did say she helped birth a baby with Willow."

"That's a good place to start," Marion agreed. "Maybe it's enough to keep those babies satisfied for the rest of the night, so I can get some sleep."

With that, she turned over on her side, snuggled down under the covers and fell asleep before Amanda turned out the light and left the room.

———————

The following Friday evening, Marion, Amanda, and Chase sat around the dining room table. Toby was at a Gambler's Anonymous 12-Step meeting but sent his regards. Marion thought he'd decided to avoid them after the long discussion with him and Chase about friendship, relationships, love, and sex. Unlike Chase, he felt guilty and mortified at unknowingly having taken advantage of Chase's curiosity.

This was a comfort food meal: fried chicken, roasted baby potatoes, green beans, and chocolate cake for dessert—the kind of meal Marion hoped would induce a natural flow of conversation.

"You have some fascinating stories in your life," Amanda said, passing the platter of chicken to Chase. "Like when you helped Willow birth a baby." She helped herself to the potatoes and passed them on. "Tell us about that."

"It was one of the 'out-world' girls. Got herself pregnant but didn't want to keep the baby but refused to kill it," Chase said as she forked out a serving of beans. "Didn't have any money, so Willow helped her."

"Out-world?" Marion asked.

"That's what we called people from outside the commune," Amanda answered. "We had our little world, our own culture on the land. The only time we interacted with people on the outside was when we'd go to market and sell our vegetables, fruits, eggs, baked goods, and cheese."

"Oh, my. Sounds very self-sustaining." *And a little cult-like*, Marion thought but didn't say.

"Yes, we were pretty much off the grid," Amanda replied.

"Where did the money go that you got from selling produce? You couldn't have needed much to survive there." Marion took a bite of crispy chicken and sighed with delight.

"I never thought to ask." Amanda looked at Chase. "Do you know where the income went?"

"Fencing, clothes, buildings, guns, I guess," Chase said.

"Guns?" Marion's eyebrows shot up.

"That would make sense," Amanda said. "The commune is pretty insular with a fence securing the perimeters. Everybody had guns back then for protection from the outside."

"What sort of buildings were there?" Marion was curious but also wanted to know what they might be facing if they made a trek east.

"People built their own houses. We had the main longhouse for communal meals and meetings. Folks lived in smaller huts, water towers, tents, and thatched-roof houses. And there were bathhouses. Not exactly up to code, if you know what I mean," Amanda said.

"Back to the baby and the out-world girl," Marion said. "Was she the only woman who came to the commune to give birth?"

"No, she was just the one I was allowed to help with. She was about my age. Willow thought she might be more comfortable with me there."

"I'm sure she was, dear," Marion said. "What about the others?"

"Sometimes two or three a week," Chase said.

Marion and Amanda exchanged startled looks.

"What became of the babies? Were they raised on the commune? There must have been an awful lot of children," Amanda said.

"No. The lady in the black car came and picked them up, took them away."

"Do you know if the lady paid Willow for birthing the babies?" Marion asked.

"I don't know. But we got a new bus to take stuff to market, a big TV for the longhouse, a new generator, and we put in a pond out in the pasture."

"Lucrative business, I'd say," Marion said under her breath to Amanda. "I think we have enough reasonable cause to plan a trip to Missouri."

"This was over thirty years ago," Amanda said. "We don't even know if Willow is still alive."

"On the chance that she is alive and has continued her business venture over the years, she needs to be stopped." Marion pounded the table with her fist, and the silverware jumped. "Those babies are howling for a reason."

"Maybe they just need their diapers changed," Chase offered.

Marion rolled her eyes and shook her head.

"I wonder if they've come into the modern era and use social media," Amanda said. "We could try a Google search or maybe Facebook."

After dinner, she excused herself and went into her bedroom to do an online search.

Chase carried the dishes to the sink, and Marion washed them.

"Chase, would you know how to install a dishwasher under the cabinet? Now that our family is enlarging, it would be a nice luxury for this old cottage. And these old hands."

"Sure," Chase said.

"How much would that cost?"

"Just the price of the materials. You feed me, and she's my mom and all."

Without thinking, Marion brought her hands to her heart and left a soapy print on her shirt. "I'm touched."

Amanda wandered back into the kitchen. "No luck," she reported. "I tried her by name and even Googled Karma Commune near Chestnutridge, Missouri. Either they're still flying under the radar, changed their name, or they no longer exist.

"I'll look up airline deals," Amanda said. "Chase, can you get a week off work? We'd like to have you with us as an eyewitness from the past. We'll cover your expenses, of course."

"Sure. I'll tell the pastor I won't be around."

———

"What if we get to Missouri and find there is no commune?" Marion asked Saturday morning.

"Well, Chase and I will have a nice little walk down memory lane—or maybe a not-so-nice one. Neither of us has great memories of the place."

"Maybe we should call the Chamber of Commerce to see if they know of the commune before we fly across the country," Marion suggested.

"Chamber of Commerce?" Amanda looked at her askance. "The town was under two hundred people back then. I can't imagine they've had a population boom that would merit one."

"Maybe the Sheriff's Department then?"

"You don't want to make this trip, do you?" Amanda said, studying Marion's face.

"It's just . . . well, we've always made these trips together. I don't know what it will be like traveling with Chase. I mean, we'll have to stay overnight, find lodging. Where will we all sleep? You both have roots that go back there; you share that. I don't. I'm not sure why—"

"May I remind you we're only doing this because a roomful of wailing babies keeps *you* awake at night?"

"You're right, I guess. I think I've been feeling a little like a third-wheel since Chase came into your life," Marion admitted.

"Into *our* life," Amanda corrected. She went into her bedroom and rebooted her computer.

"Round-trip tickets for three on American Air leaving next Friday morning from San Francisco, arriving Friday afternoon at the Springfield-Branson National Airport. We'll pick up a rental car there," Amanda announced an hour later.

"I've booked us two rooms in a little inn on our way to Chestnutridge. We'll share a room, and Chase can have some privacy. That work for you?" She stopped and glanced at Marion, who seemed overwhelmed by the barrage of information. "I figure we can take in the sights Friday night and try to find the commune Saturday morning."

"There are sights in Missouri?" Marion said.

"Oh, yeah!" Amanda waved her arms with enthusiasm. "There's the Branson Dinosaur Museum, a Hollywood Wax Museum, the Titanic. You're going to love it."

Marion raised a skeptical eyebrow.

"I forgot to tell you," Amanda said. "I ordered the DNA maternity test kit. It should arrive in a few days.

Chase and I will swab our inner cheeks, and the lab will tell us if the DNA probes match. Easy peasy," she said grinning. "Life is good."

"Good? That's not how I feel about the possibility of stumbling onto a black-market adoption ring," Marion said. "And what is our plan if we discover that Willow, or someone in the commune, is selling babies? Do you think we might be in danger? Maybe the local authorities are in on it."

"We can always call Madison if we run into trouble. He'd advise us," Amanda said.

"Oh, yes. He'd be thrilled. I'm sure he'd have some *advice* for us, alright," Marion said.

"Don't forget to call Virginia and let her know you need to go out of state. We can't have you wind up in the pokey for a parole violation," Amanda said.

Chapter 16

The Airport Express dropped the three off in front of the American Air terminal. They hauled their luggage to the curb.

"Curbside baggage check is open," Amanda called over her shoulder as she headed in that direction. "It will save us time."

"We have plenty of time." Marion's tone showcased her irritability as she struggled with a frozen wheel on her rolling tote bag. "The shuttle got us here early." She elbowed her way through the crowded sidewalk. "Where's Chase?"

Both women craned their necks and scanned the crowd. When there was a break in the flow of people, Marion spotted Chase who sat on her suitcase curbside and watched the bus pull away.

Amanda left her place in the baggage-check line and followed Marion. Both squatted down on either side of a pale-looking Chase.

"What's the matter, dear?" Marion asked.

"I've never been on an airplane," Chase said, looking morose. "I don't think I want to start today."

"You've never flown?" Marion felt flabbergasted. "How did you get to California?"

"Hitched." She stuck out her thumb. A taxi swerved to the curb, and Amanda waved him on.

"Nothing holds the plane up in the air."

After ten minutes of listening to logic, statistics on air travel safety, cajoling, pleading, Chase sat firmly with her resolve.

Marion glanced at her watch, shot a look at the terminal door, took a deep breath, and bubbled it out through her lips. She spotted a pilot headed toward the terminal entrance and charged after him. After an animated conversation, she returned with him in tow.

"This is Captain LaBlanc," she said, introducing him to Chase. "He flies airplanes. Tell her."

After a brief lecture on velocity, aerodynamics, and physics as well as a personal pledge to see to their safety, Chase allowed the captain to help her to her feet.

"Thank you, thank you, thank you," Amanda said as she pumped his hand.

"My pleasure. You folks have a good trip now," Captain LaBlanc said. He winked at Chase.

"Is the whole trip going to be like this?" Marion said sotto voce.

Once aboard the plane, Chase chose the window seat saying if she was going to die, she at least wanted to see how. Amanda had the middle, and Marion the aisle.

Chase watched with rapt attention as the steward demonstrated the art of seatbelt buckling, oxygen mask deployment, exits, and restroom locations. "In a car, you have to wear seatbelts 'cause you might crash.," Chase said as she fastened the belt.

Amanda whispered to Marion, "If we crash, seatbelts won't do us much good anyway." She then turned to Chase and explained possible air currents as sort of like potholes on the road, and that's why we wear seatbelts on a plane.

Chase shot her a skeptical look. "What if I have to pee? I'm not going to flush, that's for sure."

Amanda chuckled.

Marion shook her head, retrieved the flight magazine from the seat pocket, and skimmed through the articles. "This is going to be a long trip," she mumbled.

———

It was midday when the trio deplaned in Springfield, MO. A steady rain fell, and thick fog limited their vision to a short block beyond their rental car windshield.

"Delightful," Marion muttered, not hiding her sarcasm.

"I remember rain like this," Chase said, pressing her face to the window. "The pond would flood, and we'd have so many little frogs hopping around you couldn't walk without stepping on one.

Amanda, head hunched forward and eyes squinched in concentration said, "We'll get settled, unpack, then drive into Branson to the Titanic Museum. At least it's indoors." She flashed a quick smile over her shoulder at Marion then refocused her attention on navigating the car south on Highway 65.

"We'll pass the turnoff to Chestnutridge before we get to the inn. The commune is several miles down that road."

———

Close to an hour later, Amanda followed a sign that read The Inn of the Road. An arrow pointed over a stone bridge that crossed an ever-rising creek and dead-ended in a small gravel parking area.

The brown-shingled, slightly atilt office looked like a Tolkien hobbit house. Two rough-hewn cabins flanked the building on either side.

The rain had subsided to a drizzle, and the fog hovered in a layer above them as if stuck in the boughs of the circle of soft pines that outlined the property.

"Well, this is . . . quaint," Marion said. She opened her car door and scanned the ground for hopping frogs.

"Ah, smell this air." Amanda inhaled loudly. She stretched her arms above her head. "All the trees."

"Which little house is mine?" Chase asked.

They wandered into the office where Dot, a portly, middle-aged woman with a large mole dead-center on her ample chin, greeted them. She assigned the three to the cabin on the right with two beds, and the next cabin with a single bed. "Dinner's at six. Family style." Dot handed them their keys.

Amanda and Marion followed Chase down the stone pathway to make sure she got settled into her cabin first then brought their bags into the second cottage with two beds.

Marion chuckled as she tested the bed she'd claimed.

"What?" Amanda asked.

"The Inn of the Road? Dot with the mole? Who knew people in Missouri had a sense of humor?"

There was a loud knock at the door, and Chase stepped in.

"Can we go see the ship now? I don't remember a ship in Branson."

"You know it's not a real ship, right?" Amanda said. "It's a two-story building made to look like the hull of the Titanic. In 2006, they built this replica as a museum in honor of the 1,500 people who died when the luxury ship hit an iceberg. Most of the remains were never recovered."

"I saw the movie," Chase said.

This time Marion claimed the front seat. The view was better without the rain, and the oak and walnut tree leaves sparkled in the afternoon sun. "Look at those hills. Beautiful. Are those the Ozark mountains?"

"Well, they're not the Rockies, but they have a beauty of their own," Amanda said.

Just outside of Branson, a massive ship loomed over nearby buildings. The smokestacks—ten-stories tall—dominated the view.

"That's it, that's it." Chase bounced up and down in her seat in anticipation. She pointed to a gigantic iceberg that hung above the entrance. "Whoa, how have they kept that iceberg frozen all these years," she said, in awe. "What with the rain and all."

As Amanda parked the car, Chase bolted out of the backseat and ran over to the iceberg. She plastered herself against the white stucco phenomena and ran her hands up, down, and around the cool, bumpy, wet surface. "Iceberg, iceberg," she intoned.

The winds had kicked up a mixture of gum wrappers, leaves, twigs, bits of paper—the detritus of tourism— and splattered it across the surface.

Chase picked off the debris, one piece at a time, and deposited it into a nearby waste container. When Amanda and Marion caught up with her, she was in deep concentration.

"Chase, let's go get our tickets and tour this ship," Amanda suggested. "The museum closes at five."

"That's okay. I saw the movie." Chase continued to pick off pieces of trash and throw them into the bin. After each disposal, she caressed the surface of the iceberg and leaned her cheek against it.

"I think we've lost her," Marion commented.

"It's an Asperger's kind of thing," Amanda said. She put the price of admission in Chase's pocket and said, "If you want to come in when you're done, we'll be in the building. Just get yourself a ticket."

Once inside, they were each issued a "boarding pass" with the name of a Titanic passenger or crew member and were told they'd discover near the end if they had survived or died.

Men in double-breasted officer uniforms and women dressed as chambermaids wandered about the ship among the sounds of foghorns, clanking bells, and muffled voices.

As Marion and Amanda approached the replica of the Grand Staircase, Marion gasped. "I feel like I'm in another era. This is stunning."

At the top of the staircase, they oohed and aahed at the luxurious suites of rooms. Marion followed as Amanda wandered to the bridge that led to the Promenade Deck, a room facing a backdrop night sky sprinkled with tiny lights, reminiscent of "the final night."

The Sinking Room took them down steep sloping decks to a lifeboat. Onboard the small vessel, they dipped their fingers into a bowl of 28-degree salt water.

"A rather shocking way to realize why nearly everyone died," Marion said, shaking the water off her finger.

As it was almost five o'clock, they skipped the gift shop but found the list of survivors—neither of them had lived through the crash. "Pity to have died so young,"

Marion said. "Should we backtrack and see if Chase made it inside?"

"I have a feeling she's still working on the iceberg," Amanda said.

As they disembarked the Titanic, they found Chase sweeping wet leaves from under the edge of the iceberg with a handmade broom of twigs she'd braided together.

"I'm sorry you missed seeing the inside of the ship," Marion said.

"My work here is done." Chase sat her broom aside, wiped her hands on her slacks, stood back, and smiled in admiration at the pristine iceberg. She ran a hand gently along its surface.

"This was the best day ever," she said once they settled in the car.

Marion looked at Amanda, who merely shrugged.

They returned in plenty of time for dinner with Dot— bison stew, homemade biscuits, wilted greens, and an unexpected good quality vintage red.

"My brother ships it in from his ranch in Montana," Dot said when Marion raised her eyebrows in question about the bison.

"How thoughtful," she said. *What else could one say about bison*? she wondered.

After dinner, Dot cleared the table and brought out an apple pie, ice cream, and a pot of decaf.

Amanda and Marion regaled her with stories of their Titanic adventure.

"They have the most wonderful iceberg," Chase added wistfully.

Dot nodded, patted Chase's hand, and said, "It is a sight to behold, isn't it? So, where are you all off to tomorrow?"

"Our old stomping grounds, Karma Commune. Have you heard of it? Up near Chestnutridge?" Amanda said.

"Can't say that I have. Then again, I only bought this place six years ago. Lots of little burgs tucked away around here."

Amanda yawned. "We're pretty travel weary." She spoke for the three. "I think we'll call it a night."

They thanked Dot for dinner and her companionship and headed for their cabins.

"You going to be okay by yourself?" Amanda asked Chase.

"I'll be fine. I miss Toby."

"Of course, you do," Amanda said. "He'd be pleased to hear that. See you in the morning."

"Oh, my," Marion said when they'd settled into their beds. "I completely forgot about Toby and our life at home. Traveling disorients me, I guess. I'm sorry my passenger died on the Titanic. I'm trying not to take that personally."

"I understand," Amanda said as she clicked off the bedside lamp.

"Do you ever think about dying?" Marion asked.

"I try not to," Amanda replied. "You?"

"Often. I don't want to die alone."

"You won't. I'm here."

Chapter 17

The next morning, they shared breakfast with Dot, who'd cooked bacon, scrambled eggs, blueberry muffins, and orange juice. Afterward, the three reconnoitered in Chase's cabin to plan their attack on the commune.

"After all these years," Amanda said, "I'm sure no one would recognize us. We could say we're an alternative family scouting out intentional living communities across the country. Maybe get a tour of the place."

"Or, I could say I came back to see Willow since I grew up here," Chase offered.

"Or closer to the point," Marion said, "we could be checking out a lead our young granddaughter had been given. Say she'd heard about an 'alternative birth experience.' See how they respond."

They piled back into the rental car and headed south.

"Did you see the Chestnutridge turnoff yesterday as we drove by?" Amanda asked Chase.

Chase shook her head.

"Well, it should be about fifteen miles up the road, on the left."

Nervous energy whirled inside the car. Amanda tapped her fingers on the steering wheel and whistled tunelessly through her teeth, Marion wrung her hands in her lap and stretched her neck which made popping sounds, and Chase rocked back and forth in the backseat.

Amanda slowed and made a left turn onto a winding connector road toward Chestnutridge. They drove through a thickening of trees and along rushing creeks.

"I don't remember the road being this curvy," Amanda said. "How you doing back there?"

"You're lucky I carry peppermint Altoids," Marion said, "or we'd be stopping every few minutes." Marion popped another and practiced deep breathing.

"Chase, see if you spot the commune. I wonder if it's changed much."

Amanda slowed as they approached the area where the dirt turnoff should have been. Instead, a paved drive covered the dusty lane. No signage. No arrows. She signaled a right turn, drove in twenty feet, and stopped at a large wrought-iron gate decorated with the giant bronze letters "K" and "C." An attached fence ran deep into the woods on both sides.

"My, my," Amanda said. "Haven't we gone all fancy-schmancy." She turned off the engine, and they climbed out of the car.

Chase tried the gate. "It's locked."

"This looks like an intercom." Marion touched a round aperture covered by a grate. She pressed a button underneath.

"Karma Community. How may I help you?" a silky male voice said.

Amanda was so taken aback by all the changes, she couldn't speak. Chase stepped forward and said, "I'm Chase. I used to live here, and I want to come in."

"I'll send someone down to the gate to meet you," said the disembodied voice.

The women exchanged glances then looked through the gate. "I guess the days you just wandered in and pitched a tent are gone," Amanda said.

Moments later, a golf cart rolled up the other side of the driveway and stopped short of the gate. A middle-aged woman, with pulled back and loosely tied long chestnut-brown hair, sat in the vehicle. Dressed in a blue pantsuit with a white shell and open-toed sandals, she stepped off the cart to greet them.

"I'm Bonita Silverstone, Assistant Director of Public Affairs," she announced from the other side of the gate. "How may I help you?"

Amanda, temporarily struck mute by the difference a few decades made, stepped back and stood with her mouth agape.

"I'm Chase." Chase stepped up to the gate. "I grew up here with Willow. I came back to see the place."

Marion stepped forward, "My name is Marion. We're here from California visiting my granddaughter who is sixteen." Marion lowered her voice. "She's in a bit of bind, and I heard that your community might have a facility for her particular birthing needs. We'd like to speak with someone about that."

Bonita cocked her head to one side and narrowed her eyes. "Who did you say referred you?"

"They prefer to remain anonymous," Marion said.

"I'm afraid someone misinformed you." Bonita stepped back.

Fearing Marion had just blown their chances of getting past the gate, Amanda sparked to life. "We're thinking about relocating. I spent time here as a young adult. We're looking for an area where our 'alternative family' would be accepted. I'm Amanda, by the way."

Bonita paused. "If you'd like, park your vehicle to the side of the driveway, I'll take you to our Welcome Center." She withdrew a remote from her pocket and the gates opened with a hum. The space was just wide enough to allow the three to walk through.

Amanda relocated the car and joined Marion and Chase on the other side of the gate. With another hum, the gate slid closed and latched itself with a decisive *click*.

All three women gulped simultaneously.

Chase sat in the passenger seat of the golf cart, and Marion and Amanda squeezed into the backseat.

Sun filtered through the walnut, oak, and soft pine trees that lined the driveway. The cart's battery and a few chirping birds in the boughs were the only sounds.

Chase swiveled her head from side to side as they drove. "Where are all the cabins? I don't see any cabins. Are we in the right place? I think we might be in the wrong place, Amanda." Her voice held an edge of panic. She craned her neck toward the backseat.

"We privatized the community some years ago," Bonita said, her voice calm and soothing. "If you were here as a young person, I'm sure it looks different to you." She cast a pointed glance over her shoulder at Amanda.

"We consider ourselves an intentional community. Some former commune residents are still here, although we no longer identify with the commune lifestyle."

Amanda reached forward and put a reassuring hand on Chase's shoulder.

"How about Willow? Is she still here?" Chase asked.

"Ah, yes, Miss Willow. She lives in our infirmary now. You may visit her, but I'm not sure she will recognize you. Dementia, you know." Bonita shook her head. "Quite sad. Her daughter, Brooke, still lives in the community. Did you know her?"

Chase balled her hands into fists in her lap. "Yup."

"And, you might remember Douglas. He's one of our resident artists and is responsible for the lovely ironwork you see on the property."

"We used to call him crazy Duuuug." Amanda chuckled. "He's still alive, huh? Thought the drugs would have gotten him by now," she said.

"There are no drugs in the community," Bonita said firmly.

Amanda and Marion exchanged a look of concern. "I'm not sure this was such a good idea after all," Marion murmured. "This seems to be an entirely different place than you experienced."

"Remember, we're here for the babies," Amanda whispered.

They passed a scattering of small houses on both sides of the road. Several two-story buildings stood behind the houses. The drive ended at a large marble fountain—the kind with a peeing cherub— centered in a circular landscaped flowerbed.

Behind the fountain sat a ranch-style stucco community center with an arched doorway—the word, "Welcome," stretched across the arch with the same welded lettering as the "KC" on the outside gate.

Beyond the center, another collection of multi-family dwellings sprawled into the distance.

"Follow me, please." Bonita stepped out of the cart and led them through the archway.

"Isn't this where the longhouse was?" Chase asked Amanda. "Sure looks different. Everything's so clean."

"Yes, I believe so," Amanda said, swiveling her head to take it all in.

The Community Center seemed to be the hub of all activities. Posted at the entry, a large display board outlined the week's events, workshops, duties, and chores for the community.

"Creek and trail clearance?" Chase read. "We never used to have to clean the creek or the trails."

"They even have leadership training in community organization," Marion offered.

"Whatever happened to drum circles and fire walking?" Amanda said. "Oh, the times they are a-changing," she sang under her voice.

Bonita stopped in front of a door with a small placard attached. "Walter Bennett, Director." She tapped once and led the women into a large carpeted room with floor to ceiling windows overlooking a flagstone patio.

Mr. Bennett, behind an antique oak desk, wore a khaki suit with a white oxford shirt unbuttoned at the neck, and no tie. He came around to greet them.

"Mr. Bennett, this is Chase, Amanda, and Marion. They're visiting from California. Chase and Amanda lived here when it was Karma Commune." She arched eyebrows to imply a backstory.

They all shook hands.

"I'll leave you folks to visit. Call me when you're ready to leave," Bonita said.

Mr. Bennet ushered them into a conversational arrangement of two brown leather couches and a set of matching side chairs. Once they settled, he took a seat and said, "How may I help you?"

You could tell us about your black-market baby-selling ring, seemed inadvisable, so Amanda said,

"Everything is so different, I don't recognize the place. Maybe you could catch us up on the changes here?"

"Ah, yes." Mr. Bennett, a man of casual self-assurance, tented his fingers and rested his chin on his two index fingers.

"We are an intentional, gated community of about one hundred and twenty members. We pay monthly dues—instead of rent—to participate in maintaining this community and take part in what we have to offer."

"Which is?" Marion spoke up.

"A haven. A place without crime, drugs, alcohol. A place that nurtures individual talent and creative participation." Mr. Bennett stood, glanced out a window, and began to pace.

"We have a school, a nursery/daycare, an infirmary to care for the aged and ill, a non-denominational meditation center, and an organic garden that provides for our community meals. We even have a small cemetery to accommodate our elders who pass.

"Our farm is at the back of the property. We raise chickens and goats, and the year-round creek provides fish—our spring never runs dry." His smile showed aligned white teeth reminiscent of a Crest toothpaste ad.

"A nursery and childcare, you say?" Marion said as she sat forward in her seat on the couch. The leather creaked as if in protest. "What percentage of your residents are children?" She narrowed her eyes.

"A smaller percentage than in the past. We're mostly a middle-aged community, but occasionally, one of our residents has a baby. We like to cover all the bases."

"Seems like overkill without enough babies to utilize the space," Amanda thought out loud.

"Let me be perfectly candid, Mr. Bennett," Marion said. "We've heard that you are equipped to help pregnant young girls who cannot keep their baby. My granddaughter is in that same position. Would we be able to find the necessary accommodations here in your community?"

Amanda knew Marion had just taken a risk, but better to skip the happy sales talk and get to the point.

Mr. Bennett sat on the couch, a benign smile on his patient, stress-free face. He ran a hand through his shoulder-length, highlighted blonde hair.

"I've heard that rumor," he said, his eyes liquid with concern. "I'm not sure where it originated, or who perpetuates it, and I'm truly sorry about your granddaughter's plight. I hope you find the care she needs."

"Thank you," Marion said. "Before we leave, would it be possible to visit Miss Willow? We were told she lives in residence at the infirmary. It would mean a lot to Chase. Willow, who was then the commune's midwife, raised her from infancy."

Amanda raised her eyebrows slightly and looked for any indication that Mr. Bennett might have understood the subtext. His expression was unchanged.

"Let me see if she's up to visitors today," he said. He made a quick call and hung up the phone.

"Yes, that would be agreeable. Bonita will be here to escort you."

"I'm sure we could find our way," Amanda replied.

"I'm afraid that's not possible," Mr. Bennett said. "So nice meeting you. I hope you enjoy your stay in Missouri." With that, they were shown into the hallway.

"Is that what they call the bum's rush?" Amanda said.

"I'd sure like to get a look at that cemetery they've got on the property. Something tells me there may be some babies who came into the world and never left this place," Marion said. "I've got that crawly feeling in my head." She massaged her scalp with her fingers.

Bonita met them in the hallway and directed them out the building, down a flight of marble steps, and onto a path covered in fine, quartz-like gravel.

Jo Lauer

"Looks like something Doug would do," Chase commented. She stopped and ran her finger over the tiny bits of gravel.

"Douglas takes great pride in the aesthetics of our community," Bonita said. "All the bronze lettering you see is his work." She smiled with pride.

The path diverged. A gated hedge blocked the view to the left. They followed Bonita to the right.

"What's down that way?" Chase asked.

"Oh, that's the old cemetery. It belonged to the previous owners. This way please," Bonita said as she hurried them down the path toward the infirmary. Marion cast a longing glance then followed Bonita.

"I believe Miss Willow is in the dayroom." Bonita slid open the pocket door to a Victorian-era room flooded with light and chintz-cushioned furniture in dusty rose and antique white.

A gray-haired, wisp of a woman sat in a rocking chair near the bay window. Three guest chairs and a side table set with a tea service filled the space.

"Miss Willow? You have guests," Bonita said. "I'll be in the hallway when you've finished your visit." Bonita turned away.

"Remember now," Amanda cautioned Chase, "she may not remember you."

She's certainly not going to remember me, Amanda thought.

Willow looked up with milky-blue eyes and smiled. "Well, who do we have here?" she asked. "Have a seat." She gestured to the chairs. "Will one of you pour the tea? These old hands don't work the way they once did." She slowly wiggled her arthritic fingers.

Amanda sat, Marion poured tea, and Chase kneeled in front of the old woman and took her hands.

"These are the hands that brought me into the world. Do you remember me, Willow? I'm Chase."

Tears welled in Willow's eyes as she studied Chase's face. "Of course, I remember you, child. I never knew what happened to you after you ran off."

She leaned forward and wrapped her thin arms around Chase. "You were like a daughter to me."

Chase sat down beside her.

They all sipped their tea and delayed the uncomfortable conversation that needed to happen next.

Amanda cleared her throat. "I don't know if you remember me, Willow. I'm Amanda. My husband and I lived at Karma for a while many years ago. I got pregnant, he left, and you delivered my baby."

Willow crooked her head and studied Amanda. "I delivered so many babies back then," she said.

"Sometimes more than one a day. I wish I could tell you I remember your situation, but . . ." She shook her head slowly.

"That's what we wanted to speak with you about," Marion said, setting her teacup back on the table.

"You told me my baby was stillborn, and you took her away before I got to see her," Amanda said, blinking back tears.

"Oh, I'm so sorry, dear," Willow said. "We didn't have good medical care on the commune, and many babies didn't make it through birth if there were complications." She lowered her head in remorse.

It was time to decide. Amanda could pursue her lost-baby cause, probably with no useful outcome. Willow's memory had faded. The DNA test waiting at home would confirm her connection with Chase.

"The other babies, all those babies you brought into the world." Amanda chose her words carefully. "Were they all from people living on the commune? I don't remember that many pregnant women."

Willow smiled. "Of course not, dear. They were girls from . . ." Willow placed a trembling hand over her pale lips. "We're not supposed to speak of those days. Ever," she said. She picked up her teacup splashing tea onto her lap. "*Oh!*" she cried.

Chase took the cup from her hands, dabbed the moisture up with a napkin, and held her hand.

"It's okay," she murmured. "It's just us. You can tell us. We're family."

Willow turned her milky gaze on Chase. "They took them away, you know. But I kept you. You were mine. Brooke was spiteful. They should have taken her."

A tap on the door interrupted the conversation.

"How's our visit going?" Bonita asked as if speaking to a room of children. "Are we ready to let Miss Willow have her rest time?" She nodded with encouragement.

"I'd like to use the restroom before we leave if I might," Marion said. "The tea and all . . ." She leaned toward Amanda and whispered, "Cover for me."

"Of course. Right this way," Bonita said. "Just down the hall on your right. Can you find your way back?"

"Yes, thank you. Oh, and a tea spillage in the parlor could use your attention."

———

Marion listened as Bonita's footsteps retreated then faded. Marion slipped out of the bathroom and out the rear exit. As quickly as she could, she followed the path back around to where it split.

At the cemetery gate, Marion jiggled the lock, which fell loose and she eased through the opening.

Unattended marked graves scattered throughout. Grass, weeds, and the detritus from overhanging trees covered brick markers. She brushed one grave free of debris. *Coyote. 1980.*

At the back, she saw a small plot separated by a row of large river stones. On closer inspection, Marion counted twenty-four smaller stones, closely spaced, with no other marking.

That's enough proof for me, she thought and hurried down the path to the infirmary.

Just as she stepped into the hallway, Bonita came out of the bathroom.

"Where were you?" Her voice was sharp and accusatory. "I thought I should check on you. It's been a while."

"Yes, yes. Sorry," Marion said as she walked up to Bonita. "I'm afraid I got disoriented. I guess I'm not used to all this traveling." She gave Bonita a feeble old-lady smile. "We should be going."

"We don't allow visitors free access to our community," Bonita said. She took Marion's arm with more force than was necessary. "I'll escort you back to the dayroom."

They gathered up Amanda and Chase and said their goodbyes to Willow, who wrung her hands as though agitated.

"I don't suppose we could see the nursery before we go?" Amanda said.

"I'm afraid not. It's getting late. I hope you enjoyed your visit."

In front of the Welcome Center, they boarded the golf cart and headed back to the main gate.

"Thank you for everything," Marion said.

"Our pleasure. Do revisit us if you're ever in the area," Bonita said. The crispness of her words belied her invitation.

The gate opened and clicked firmly once the three were on the outside. They climbed into the rental car and drove down the driveway.

Amanda turned off the ignition before entering the road. "I need a moment," she said. "That whole experience was surreal."

"We were so close before Willow got frightened. She has more information," Marion said. "And I think Bonita suspects something."

"Willow remembered me," Chase said, her voice small.

An old Chevy pickup truck slowed and turned from the road into the drive. The driver nodded at them as he drove past.

"Good God," said Amanda. "Is that Doug's old pickup?" She craned her neck. Impulsively, she honked her horn. The pickup slowed to a stop, then backed until it was even with the rental. Both drivers rolled down their windows.

"Doug? Is that you?" Amanda leaned out her window to inspect the aged face of a man with wild gray dreadlocks and a stubble beard.

"Welcome, visitors. Were you here to check out our community?" he said, his voice gravelly.

Chase rolled down her window and leaned forward. "Doug, it's me, Chase. Do you remember me? I used to help you gather river stones for the bury patch," she said. She turned to the front seat and said, "That's what we used to call the graveyard."

Doug opened his door and stepped out. "Chase? My little runaway?"

Chase climbed out of the backseat, and although she seemed to stiffen up like a board, she allowed herself to be swept into a bearhug by the burly man.

Both Amanda and Marion got out of the car and greeted him.

"Do you remember Amanda?" Chase asked. "She used to live here. And this is Marion."

They shook hands.

"Amanda, Amanda." Doug rolled the name around for a moment. "Were you the pregnant gal who ran off after giving birth or something? Yeah, I remember you."

"I'm surprised," Amanda said, grinning, "given the times and all."

"Yeah," Doug chuckled. "Well, I got clean when the place changed hands some time ago. It was either get sober or move off the land and die, I guess. Didn't think I could survive anywhere else if you know what I mean."

Amanda nodded.

"Doug, we've been trying to get some information about the early days of Karma and how things currently run. I'm afraid we've hit a roadblock," Marion said.

"Mr. B. stonewall you, did he? The guy needs to loosen up."

"And Bonita, as well," Marion said.

"That gal just needs a good . . ." Doug dropped his head and mumbled, "Sorry, ma'am. That was inappropriate."

Amanda stifled a chuckle.

"Would it be possible to chat for a while? I think you might be able to shed some light on our search," Marion said.

"Got a community meeting coming right up," he said, "but if you come back tomorrow, we can meet in my cottage. I'll be glad to talk to you."

"Yes, thank you," Marion said.

"See you tomorrow," Amanda added.

Doug reached over and ruffled Chase's hair as if she were still the kid he remembered.

They got in their vehicles and headed their separate directions.

"That was an act of fate," Amanda said. "If I hadn't stopped to catch my breath, we would have missed him."

Marion agreed. "This might be just the break we need."

Filled with optimism and good cheer, they headed back for a late lunch with Dot.

————

"I noticed you got a little misty-eyed when Chase and Willow reunited after all those years. Were you upset about their bond?" Marion said as they were getting ready for bed,

Amanda sighed. "It occurred to me that Willow is the only mother-type figure Chase ever had."

"Until now," Marion said.

Amanda smiled at her. "I guess I was a pinch envious of their connection and—"

"And?"

"And jealous that I never had much of a connection with the woman who gave birth to me."

"I'm sorry about that," Marion said as she crawled into her bed.

"Yeah, well, that's life." Amanda clicked off the lamp next to her bed.

Chapter 18

The next morning, Dot packed a picnic lunch for them.

"The way to Doug's heart, I'm pretty sure, is through fried chicken and chocolate cupcakes," Amanda said with a chuckle. "Thanks, Dot. See you later," they called as they pulled back out onto the highway.

The sun released the fragrance of the pines, and they drove with their windows down to breathe in the fresh mountain air.

"I have a good feeling about this," Amanda said.

"You don't think Doug's loyalty to the community will be a problem? Sounds like they saved his life," Marion said.

"Too much wind! Too much wind! Roll up the windows, quick!" Chase shrieked from the backseat. Her hands covered her ears, and she leaned so her body rested on her thighs.

"Sorry, Chase," Amanda said as she and Marion rolled their windows up. "Just never know what too much stimulation is going to look like," she said, glancing over at Marion.

Chase sat up and looked around with caution. "Too much wind," she stated matter-of-factly.

Marion gobbled a few more Altoids as they drove toward Chestnutridge. At the Karma Community driveway, Amanda slowed down and noted a blue Toyota had pulled into the visitor's parking space.

Three people emerged, a middle-aged man, who carried himself as if much older, a woman who appeared slightly younger, and a pregnant girl somewhere in early adolescence. They walked to the gate and stood there as if waiting.

Within moments, Bonita drove up in her golf cart. After a brief conversation, the guests passed through the sliding gate, which clicked shut behind them.

Amanda pulled forward and turned off the ignition. "Hi Bonita, Amanda here," she said with a big smile as she approached the gate.

"Of course," Bonita said. "How may I help you?"

"We're here to see Doug. We ran into him while leaving yesterday, and he asked us to come back today for a visit."

"I'm sorry," Bonita said. "Douglas has been called away."

"Called away?" Marion had gotten out of the car and joined Amanda at the gate. "When will he be back?"

"I'm not sure," Bonita said. Her face was implacable.

"Where did he go?" Amanda asked.

"I'm not at liberty to say. You'll have to excuse me; I need to take our guests in." With that, she turned and shuttled her cargo down the path.

"Can you believe that?" Amanda huffed. "I don't buy that for one minute. I bet they locked him up somewhere so he couldn't talk to us."

"Where's Doug?" Chase asked when the two returned to the car. "He said he wanted to see us."

"Bonita said he's gone," Amanda said.

"Let's not get paranoid. It's unfortunate Doug's not here, but why would Bonita lie? She didn't know we were coming to see him, or about what," Marion reasoned.

"What's that?" Chase said, pointing to a small object embedded in the tree next to the fence that had caught her attention.

Amanda and Marion looked up. "I didn't notice that yesterday," Marion said.

"Well, I'll be damned," Amanda muttered. "It's a surveillance camera. Paranoid, huh?"

"The way it's angled, they could have seen us talking with Doug yesterday. Perhaps they questioned him and decided it was against their best interest to have him talk with us today," Marion said. "Sorry about the paranoid thing."

"They holding him prisoner?" Chase said.

"I don't know, kiddo. But what I do know is that a pregnant girl just went into their facility, and I'll bet you dollars-to-donuts she won't be driving back out with that man and woman."

"We have a picnic basket full of food," Marion said. "I say we do some surveillance of our own. Let's park outside the drive and wait for them to come out."

"If it's just the two of them, we take down the license plate number . . . maybe follow them for a little while." Amanda started the car, turned it around, and headed back toward the highway. She backed into a small pull-off just to the left of the driveway and cut the engine.

"Chase, be our scout. See if you spot any more of those cameras up in the trees, would you?" Amanda said.

Chase scoured the bordering trees and reported they were in the clear. "Let's eat," she said, rubbing her hands together in anticipation.

"If they're just dropping her off, checking her in, doing paperwork, whatever," Marion said, "it shouldn't be more than an hour or so." She passed around the paper plates and napkins, then the chicken, potato salad, carrot sticks, and chocolate cupcakes.

The car filled with wonderful smells and the sounds of agitated maceration, contemplative chewing, and reckless chomping. When they'd finished lunch, they looked out the windows at the clear sky, the sporadic traffic, the towering trees. No one seemed inclined toward conversation.

Less than thirty minutes passed when the car with the man and woman approached the highway, stopped, then made a cautious right turn. The pregnant girl was nowhere to be seen.

Marion grabbed her purse, extracted a pen and tablet, and wrote down the license number. Amanda attempted to switch on the ignition. After a grinding sound, the engine didn't catch.

"Well, crap!" Amanda said. "Figures." She drummed her fingers on the steering wheel.

"The car has out-of-state license plates," Marion said. "It shouldn't be too hard to find. Surely, they're staying nearby."

"What are we going to do?" Chase called from the backseat.

"First, we're going to get this car running," Amanda said.

"Then what?" Chase said.

Then what, indeed, Amanda thought. Even if they could find the couple, why would the man and woman, who dropped off their child to give birth to a baby, talk with perfect strangers if they knew the baby would be swept away into an illegal adoption ring?

"Uh, oh," Marion said.

Amanda glanced over at her.

"What if . . . bear with me now; I'm just thinking out loud. What if the community has ties with a legal, private adoption agency, and no crime is being committed?" Marion offered. "They could have gone legit when they brought the property and saw the need that was being met illegally, right?"

"You forget about those crying babies that keep you awake night after night," Amanda reminded her. "If it's all on the up-and-up, why all the upset? Why would they come to you?"

"I guess you're right," Marion conceded.

Amanda prayed to a God she didn't believe in and tried the ignition again. This time it caught. Coincidence, she thought with a shake of her head.

"We'll head toward Branson. Keep your eyes peeled."

Marion scanned street signs as they crept up the road. "There's a sign for a motel, next street. Let's give it a try."

"What do we have to lose?" Amanda signaled a right-hand turn and inched passed several businesses.

"There! There's the Toyota. Now what?" Marion asked.

They sat in silence for a moment.

"I suppose we could wait them out. They have to leave sometime," Amanda offered.

"Another stakeout?" Chase called from the backseat. "But, we're out of food."

"If we get desperate, there's a diner on the corner. Maybe they'll decide to have dinner there?" Amanda drove by the motel, made a U-turn, and parked within view of the motel's parking lot.

"I have to pee," Chase said.

"I could use a cup of coffee," Marion said. "Let's leave the car here and walk to that diner."

"Wow! Looks like it's been around since the 50s. Check out the neon 24-hour OPEN sign."

"I want a chocolate malt!" Chase shouted.

Once in the restaurant, they marveled at the soda counter with cool red stools, the table-top silver jukeboxes, and the long list of malts.

"Can I get you all a booth?" the waitress, her red hair tied back in a ponytail said with a snap of her chewing gum.

"Window seat, please," Marion replied. "So we can see if they leave," she whispered to Amanda and Chase.

The waitress brought them to a large booth next to the window and passed out menus. "My name's Marcelle," she introduced herself. "Coffee all around?"

"I'd like a chocolate malt," Chase said.

"We just happen to make the best malts in Missouri," Marcelle said with a wink. "Be right back."

Me too," Chase said. She excused herself and headed for the bathroom.

The threesome dawdled over their drinks and cast surreptitious glances down the street.

It was late afternoon when Marcelle checked in on them again.

"Can I get you anything else?" she said, having refilled the coffee cups multiple times.

"No, thank you. Let's get going," Marion said.

They paid the bill and left. Halfway down the sidewalk, Amanda spotted the couple leaving the motel and strolling toward them.

"Uh, oh, what do we do now?" Amanda threw a panicked glance at Marion.

"Keep walking. I'll handle this," Marion said.

"Oh, hello," Marion said as the couple approached. "Didn't we see you just down the road a while ago?"

"Why, yes. I believe you did," the woman stammered.

"How fortunate is this?" Marion introduced the trio. "We were hoping to have a word with you, and here you are!" She sounded positively delighted. Amanda and Chase beamed.

"You were?" The woman's voice was wary. She regarded the women as if they were in clown suits. "I'm Jennifer Long, and this is my husband, Archie," she said.

They all shook hands.

"Um, I suppose that would be alright," As if hesitant, Jennifer glanced at Archie who nodded. "We were just going to have a little dessert and coffee. Won't you join us?"

"Table for five?" Marcelle said with a look of surprise. "Back so soon? You must love our coffee."

"The malts," Chase blurted.

After a few awkward minutes of page-flipping the menus and decision-making, Jennifer seemed to appraise the women once again.

"What exactly do you want to speak with us about?" Jennifer asked.

Amanda unfolded the long story, starting with her experience at Karma Commune, the stillbirth of her daughter, and Chase's appearance in her life. Then, she explained Marion's psychic gifts that allowed the dead and traumatized to speak to her.

Archie wore his skepticism like a too-tight necktie.

Amanda concluded her story with their choice to make a trip back to Missouri to see if the suspected illegal activity was still going on.

"Oh, my," was all Jennifer said at the end of the tale.

"Are you saying we're involved in an illegal adoption?" Archie spoke up for the first time.

"We certainly hope not," Marion said.

"But we find it suspicious that Mr. Bennett denied any connection with the 'unfortunate rumor' about the community providing any such services," Amanda added. "And yet, here you are." She gestured across the Formica table.

"And that they have a nursery facility, although the average age of their community members is around forty," Marion added.

"And, I can assure you that Marion's psychic gifts have helped us solve a handful of mysteries over the last couple of years." Amanda closed her menu and peered directly at Jennifer. "Those babies are crying for a reason."

Marion smiled her appreciation.

Archie chewed his bottom lip. "I'm not comfortable with this conversation," he said. "I think we should excuse ourselves." He moved to scoot his chair away from the table.

"Oh, please." In desperation, Marion grabbed his wrist. "Just a few more questions. This is important to us."

"What can it hurt, Archie?" Jennifer said. "We need to know if we're getting in over our heads. Julie's due in two days. We could still get her back if we needed to."

Archie glared at Marion who immediately released his wrist. With grumbling resignation, he sat back in his chair.

"I'm sorry," Jennifer apologized. "This has been a stressful time. I'm sure you can understand. What else can we tell you?"

"Did you sign any nondisclosure or privacy agreement?" Marion asked.

"Yes, of course," Jennifer said. "The adoptive parents wished to remain anonymous, and of course, so did we."

"Can you tell us how you heard about the community?"

Jennifer glanced at Archie, who gave a small resigned nod.

"We live just over the state line in Iowa. A small town, very conservative. Our local church community is like an extended family." Archie nodded slowly. He folded his hands on the table and looked thoughtfully at his wife.

"We're good Christian people," Jennifer said. "When Julie—that's our daughter, she's only fifteen—found herself, well, um, pregnant." Jennifer sighed; her shoulders dropped. "We didn't know what to do. We don't believe in abortion. We're not equipped to raise another child, and Julie is in her last year of middle school."

Amanda and Marion nodded their sympathy and understanding.

"And the boy's family?" Marion asked.

"They were in the process of moving to New York and didn't want their son's future 'ruined' by this event. He was also fifteen," Jennifer said.

"Our assistant pastor said he'd heard of a place where Julie could have her baby, receive good care, and the adoption would be handled without our involvement." She stopped to take a ragged breath.

"The price was fairly affordable, so we met with the community's director last month and made arrangements to check in our daughter the week she was due."

Archie now sat with his head in his hands. "I hope we're doing the right thing," he mumbled.

"I think it might be time to take this to the authorities," Marion said.

"Oh, no," Jennifer protested. "Are we going to get in trouble? I want Julie to get through this experience and put it behind her. Couldn't you wait until after we leave?"

"This is a perfect opportunity to put someone on the case right away, to follow up on what happens to a baby after birth. They'll likely need to interview your daughter afterward," Marion said. "I'm sorry. I know this isn't at all what you had in mind."

"We'll be sure the investigators know you were not aware of illegal activity," Amanda said. She turned to

Marion. "I think we should go back to the inn and place a call to Madison."

"Oh, dear. I'm not looking forward to that," Marion said under her breath.

They exchanged contact information with the Longs and promised to stay in touch with updates as things unfolded.

Back in the car, Chase, who'd sat quietly through the meeting, said, "I'm glad no one sent me away when I was born."

"I'm glad too," Amanda said. She reached between the seats and squeezed Chase's hand.

Chapter 19

Back at the inn, Chase headed out to explore the property while Marion and Amanda called Madison. They sat on Marion's bed and put him on speakerphone.

"Madison Bright," he answered with his familiar, no-nonsense greeting.

"Madison, hello. It's Amanda and Marion. You're on speakerphone."

"Ah, to what do I owe this dubious pleasure?"

Over their time working cases together, they had either evolved or devolved—Marion was never sure which—to something resembling sibling rivalry, with Madison attempting to hold on to his professional status as a detective while being relegated to little-brother status in their eyes.

"We need your help," Marion said.

"We're in the Ozarks," Amanda added.

"The *Ozarks*?" They could envision him slapping his forehead. "Dare I ask?"

"We'll save you the trouble," Amanda said. "We think we've come upon a black-market, baby-selling ring just outside Chestnutridge, Missouri."

"Come upon?" Madison said.

"Well, it all started back home in California," Marion said. "We thought we might spare you the details and ask if you could intervene with the local authorities. Get permission for us to investigate the upcoming birth of a child."

"I'm almost certain I know the answer to this already, but why are you not going directly to police yourselves?"

"It all started with dead babies crying all night and keeping Marion awake," Amanda said.

"I know I'm going to regret this, but I probably need the whole story." They heard a weary sigh on the other end of the line.

From start to finish—much like peeling an onion layer by layer—they took turns telling him the details which included the suspicious graveyard on the property. Occasionally he interrupted to ask for clarification.

Forty minutes later, Madison said, "Just to be clear; you want me to call the Branson officials, relay a shortened—much shortened—version of this story, and ask them to investigate?"

"Yes," Marion said. "Time is of the essence. Julie is due to give birth the day after tomorrow."

"And unfortunately, we're scheduled to leave tomorrow morning, so we can't stay and see this through," Amanda said.

"How unfortunate for the locals," Madison said.

"Am I hearing sarcasm in your voice?" Marion asked.

There was a long pause.

"Alright," Madison said. "If this is what you think it is, you need to step away, starting now. I'm serious. I've got your contact information and the Longs'. I expect you'll hear from the officials down there. But for now, I want you on a plane headed back home."

"Nice to know you miss us," Amanda said.

"I feel such a weight off my heart," Marion said when they hung up.

"How do you suppose they're going to investigate this?" Amanda's voice held intense excitement. "Wouldn't it be fun to—"

"Hands off," Marion interrupted with a shake of her head. "We leave tomorrow."

"Yes, but we have the rest of the afternoon," Amanda said.

Marion grounded the implication with a glare. The idea didn't even get to taxi down the runway.

That morning, the day before they'd leave, Dot asked Chase what she'd like for dinner. When they walked through the office and into the dining room that evening, the aroma of pot roast, mashed potatoes, corn on the cob, green beans, and chocolate cake kissed their noses.

"Can't tell you how nice it's been having you folks stay with me," Dot said. "Gets lonely in-between bookings." She smiled at Chase. "And I just love cooking for a gal who has a good appetite."

"Thanks, Aunt Dot," Chase said.

"Aunt Dot?" both Amanda and Marion said at once.

"Figured I'd start building my family. I've got Willow as my grandmom since she's so old. You as my mom," she nodded at Amanda, "and Marion as my bonus-mom. And then, Toby back home wants to be my husband someday. Doug probably would have been my uncle if I'd asked. Might as well have an aunt in there." She grinned happily.

Dot's eyes filled with tears as she said, "I'd be honored to be your aunt. You can come back and visit any old time, you hear?"

After a lighthearted dinner conversation, they played a rousing game of Mexican Dominoes.

"We'll be up before the sun tomorrow," Amanda said. "Okay if we just leave the keys in our rooms, so we don't wake you?"

"You sure you don't want a little breakfast before you go?" Dot said.

"We'll catch something at the airport," Marion offered. "Thanks for everything, Dot. You've been such a lovely hostess."

With hugs all around and promises to stay in touch, they called it a night.

———————

They had an uneventful flight back to California. At the airport, they picked up some Mc breakfasts and ate them on the plane. Chase claimed the aisle seat, so she'd be closer to the exit if they crashed. Marion took the middle and finished the novel she'd brought along. Amanda snoozed leaning against the window.

On the drive home to Sonoma County, each woman reflected on what she'd missed while they adventured in Missouri.

"I missed seeing Toby," Chase said. "He makes me happy inside. And I miss painting. The library at the church needs a fresh coat of paint. Can't wait to get started."

"I missed cooking. Even though Dot spoiled us terribly, there's something about having free range of my kitchen," Marion said. "And I missed choir. I think I also missed a performance. Shoot," she said in hindsight. "I wonder if they'll let me back in?"

"I missed puttering around the house," Amanda said. "Guess it's fair to say, we're glad to be home."

They pulled into the driveway. Chase's truck was parked out front. She got out of the car, ran over to her vehicle, leaned over, and pressed her cheek onto the hood. "I've missed you," she said. "You're nice and warm from the sun."

Marion watched Chase and recalled her passion for the iceberg at the Titanic. "I may never understand her, but I've learned to appreciate her," she said as Amanda unloaded their suitcases from the trunk.

Amanda opened the mailbox and extracted several days' worth of junk mail, bills, notices, and an official-looking envelop from Brickland Laboratories, which she clasped to her chest.

"Chase, come on in the house a minute before you take off," Amanda called.

They all tromped into the living room. "Have a seat," Amanda said. "I think I have some good news to share." She beamed at Chase.

As she tore open and quickly scanned the letter, the light of excitement in her eyes went out, and she sunk into the nearest chair.

"Oh, no," she said, shaking her head slowly.

"Is it the DNA results?" Marion asked, leaning forward, her lips pressed tightly together.

"There's no match," Amanda murmured. She looked as dejected as an abandoned pup.

Marion hugged her. "I'm so sorry."

"Is that the good news?" Chase said, fidgeting.

"No, honey," Amanda said. "That means I'm not your biological mom." Tears glistened in her eyes.

"Does that mean I have to go home now?" Chase wrinkled the edge of her shirt and tapped her foot against the hardwood floor.

"No, no, of course not," Amanda reassured her. "I'm not much of a prize, but if you'll have me, I'll be your chosen mom. Nothing's changed there. We're still your family, okay?"

"Okay." Chase blinked. "I'm going to go see Toby now," she said. "See you Friday night." With that, she picked up her suitcase and carried it to her truck.

"Oh, Amanda," Marion said, her voice choked with compassion. "That means you still don't know if your daughter died at birth or was adopted out."

"I guess it also means Chase was someone else's baby that Willow decided to keep. What a mess." Amanda's expression was crestfallen. "I need to go lie down for a bit." She heaved herself up from the chair.

"Yes, of course. You do that. We'll talk later."

———

Two hours later, Amanda returned to the living room looking restored, if not revitalized.

"I've been thinking," Amanda said. "I guess we owe Audrey Cuthbert a big thank you for dying."

"I beg your pardon?"

"Well, think about it. If she hadn't died, we wouldn't have met Toby, who we introduced to Chase. Without Chase, there'd be no reason to research my past and the commune. Those babies would not have contacted you. And no trip to Missouri to helped bust up an illegal baby-selling ring would have ensued." Amanda smiled and tilted her head at Marion. "Don't you ever think about those kinds of connections in life?"

"Not really. But I'm glad you do . . . I think."

"Like, what if I'd never even lived on the commune? Never had a baby? What if we'd never met?" she asked.

"Okay," Marion said, "I'll play. What if Audrey *hadn't* died? We'd still have our comfortable, tidy little life. That trip exhausted me."

"I think 'tidy' is highly overrated," Amanda said. "Come on; let's have dinner."

———

A week later, back into their familiar routine, Amanda sat at the kitchen table and thumbed through an electrical engineering book as she finished her coffee. "Who was that on the phone?" she asked when Marion came into the kitchen.

"Stony," she said.

"Have you been drummed out of choir for missing a performance?" Amanda smiled around the rim of her cup.

"Quite the contrary," Marion said. "He wanted to make sure I got home safely and to remind me of tonight's rehearsal." She noted the book Amanda was perusing, *Electronics for Dummies*. "There's a class at the Senior Center on household wiring," she said.

"I don't want to go near that Center for a while. It's like a magnet for bad experiences." Amanda shrugged. "I'm going to pretend I've adjusted to retirement and don't need something to fill my time."

"But what will you do with yourself all day?"

"That's just it. I don't want to *do* anything."

"B . . . b . . . but . . ." Marion sputtered. "Your brain will go to mush, your hair will thin, and your teeth will fall out."

"My teeth will fall out?"

"You know what I mean. We're at the 'use it or lose it' stage of life. Look at Audrey. S*he* was an active senior."

"She's dead," Amanda reminded Marion.

Before the conversation could degenerate even further, the phone rang. It was Madison Bright requesting a meeting with them down at the precinct.

"Should we call Chase?" Marion wondered out loud.

"I think she'd probably rather be with Toby," Amanda said. "We can fill her in later,"

———

"You're looking well, Madison," Marion said after they'd settled themselves around the scarred wooden table in Interview Room 3.

"It seems you two have stirred up quite a hornet's nest," he said, skipping over the small talk and the compliment. "I want you to know that I risked my professional credibility by explaining the situation you two found yourselves in."

His scowl carried little punch.

"Sorry about that," Amanda said with a grin. "We could have tried busting it open ourselves, but . . ."

"No. No, you made the right call," Madison admitted. "Here's the preliminary update—more to follow. Surveillance was set up to follow the baby immediately after birth. The infant was taken to Kentucky and placed with a family who had six children, all living on state aid."

"They crossed state lines?" Amanda noted.

"That they did. Apparently, they thought it was worth the risk. It wasn't."

"What about Julie, is she alright?" Marion asked.

"Yes. She agreed to be available for follow-up interviews if necessary. Neither she nor her parents are liable for any wrongdoing. They paid for her delivery and aftercare and believed the community when they were told an independent, legitimate adoption would follow."

"And the family in Kentucky bought the baby?" Amanda said. "Lucrative business."

"A second 'transaction' was discovered when a young woman from Honduras flew to the commune and paid to give birth. She added more cash to have both the baby and her listed as U.S. citizens on the birth certificate—she figured this would assure her of citizenship."

"Oh, dear," Marion said. "That makes it an international crime."

"It does. The FBI raided the community's safe and found a file cabinet full of records going back to when the property changed hands six years ago. Mr. Bennet, Ms. Silverstone, and Brook, with no last name, are all looking at prison sentences."

Amanda sat back as if the wind had been knocked out of her.

"Were there any records from earlier?" Marion asked, glancing at a very pale Amanda.

"No, apparently no records were kept when the place was a commune."

Amanda shook her head. "I guess not all mysteries are solvable," she said under her breath as she reflected on her past. "What will become of the community? Will they get shut down?"

"It's not illegal to have an intentional community," Madison said. "There will be ongoing investigations into the births, but there's no indication that shows anyone

else was involved in the baby scam. I guess they'll limp along without a leader."

"Which might the best thing that could happen," Amanda said, thinking of Doug's assessment of the staff. "Everyone will look out for everyone else, like the old days." Her eyes softened with nostalgia.

"What about the cemetery?" Marion asked. "My hunch is there are a lot of babies who didn't make it buried there."

"Exhuming bodies is a whole other process," Madison said. "They're on it. It's not all tidied up yet, by a long shot."

"A wise woman once said, 'Tidy is highly overrated,'" Marion said.

Chapter 20

"So that's the update," Amanda said, filling in Chase and Toby. The family, as Amanda had begun to think of this conglomeration of individuals, was gathered around the dining room table for their now-traditional Friday night dinner.

"Don't you wonder what would have happened if the place hadn't changed hands?" Toby said. "I mean maybe Willow—is that her name?" He consulted Chase who nodded. "Maybe she was selling babies back then."

"It's likely," Amanda said, "considering all the improvements made in the later years. God knows, none of us had any money."

"As you've said . . ." Marion reached over and patted Amanda's hand. "Not all mysteries are solvable."

"The good news is that you haven't been plagued by screaming babies and have slept through the night," Amanda said.

Marion nodded. "There's that," she said.

"Toby, what's new in your life?"

"I'm going to be a dad," he said with a huge grin.

Marion gasped and grabbed her heart, and Amanda's fork clattered to the table as her hand fell onto her plate. Peas scattered onto the table.

Chase sat impassively.

"I'm adopting this little mongrel puppy from the Humane Society," Toby said. "My aunt's house has a great backyard—perfect for a dog to run around in."

"We're calling him Bert," Chase added.

When Amanda and Marion recovered from their misunderstanding, Amanda said, "Please, don't ever begin a sentence like that again."

"And," Toby continued, "I asked Chase to move in with me."

"Don't go rolling your peas again," Chase said, looking at Amanda. "I said 'no.'"

Toby looked downcast.

She glanced at Toby. "As much as I like you and missed you while I was gone, I just don't think I'm ready to live full time with someone."

Toby nodded, resigned. "I guess I knew that. But when you are, I'll be here."

Chase nodded.

"That's my girl," Amanda said with a wink.

———

The next morning Amanda pushed the lawn-mower around a patch of grass in the front yard.

The postal lady walked up to Amanda's mailbox. "Morning."

"Morning, Geraldine," Amanda called. "Did you bring my lottery-winner notice today?"

"Amanda, you've got to play the danged game if you expect to win," Geraldine bantered back.

"I do have a letter from the Colonoscopy Clinic, though. I brought you one a couple weeks ago. You're not avoiding them, are you?" She came up the walk and handed Amanda the day's mail.

"You are not my mother," Amanda said. She took the mail and placed the notice on the bottom.

"And thank goodness for that," Geraldine replied. "Have a good day." With that, she walked across the street.

Amanda went inside and sat on the couch to sort the mail.

"Anything interesting?" Marion sat down next to Amanda.

"Not unless you find bills fascinating," Amanda said. "Whoa, what's this? Are you taking *Playboy* now?"

"What? Let me see that." Marion took the magazine from Amanda. "This is more your style than mine."

"Geraldine must have mixed in some of John's mail." She turned the magazine over and read the name and address on the back. "Yup."

"I'll walk it across the street," Marion said. She inadvertently bumped Amanda's arm, and the remaining mail fell to the floor. She bent to pick it up.

"What's this?" she said, picking up the envelope from the Colonoscopy Clinic. "Weren't you supposed to make an appointment last month?"

"Geez, what's with you and Geraldine? Can't a girl have a little privacy?"

"Not if that girl ignores a critical appointment request," Marion said, shaking her head.

"I made the appointment if you must know." Amanda took the envelope from Marion and opened it.

"Well?" Marion said. She craned her neck and saw the words "Second Notice" in red.

"It's nothing," Amanda said. "Something about the results. They want me to come back in."

"The office is still open. Why don't you call and make an appointment now, while you're thinking about it?"

"You're not my mother," Amanda heard herself say the second time in less than ten minutes. What's with the adolescent rebellion, she wondered?

"And I hope you'll always remember that," Marion retorted.

"Fine." Amanda stormed into her bedroom to make the call in private.

"This is Amanda Pritchard," she said into the phone. "I'm calling because I got a follow-up letter saying something about an *irregular* outcome. Can you tell me what that means?" She waited a moment.

"Tomorrow? Geez, let me think. Um, okay, I guess. See you at two o'clock." She set the phone down on her bedside table and collapsed onto the bed. She had trouble catching her breath, and her heart beat felt erratic.

When Amanda was ten, her grandmother, the only person she'd been close to, died from colon cancer. The loss was even more traumatic because no one ever spoke of her again. It was as if an unspoken curse on the family would befall if anyone ever said Grandma Lottie's name aloud.

A cold sweat broke out on her forehead. "Please God," she said to a deity she didn't believe in. "Not that."

Amanda was quiet through dinner and turned in early saying she had a headache.

Marion knew not to push her.

Around three o'clock the next afternoon, Amanda came in the front door and headed straight for the couch. She plunked down, kicked off her shoes, and leaned back. Her body, which had felt so heavy that morning, now felt light, buoyant.

Marion came in from the kitchen. "Well?" she said, sitting down beside Amanda. "What's the verdict?"

"Looks like I'm going to be around a while," she said with a grin. "Just benign cysts and they'll remove them."

"Oh, I'm so grateful." A wave of relief crossed Marion's face. "Life without my best friend is unthinkable."

"I'll just have to get yearly check-ups," Amanda said, "and that's okay by me."

"Now that we know you're going to live, maybe you could finish that patch of unmowed grass out there?"

———

Lost in thought, Amanda pushed the mower back and forth. Once finished, she came back into the house to find Marion at the dining room table. A 500-piece jigsaw puzzle lay in disarray in the center. The picture on the lid was of Monet's *Water Lilies*.

"Care to join me?" Marion said. "It's supposed to be good for the brain."

"You couldn't pay me enough to do a jigsaw puzzle," Amanda said with a chuckle. "We are different in so many ways. Will you marry me?"

Marion shot Amanda a wide-eyed look of disbelief.

"I know, I know . . ." Amanda said. "Just hear me out." She took a chair opposite Marion and leaned over the puzzle pieces.

"That colonoscopy scare got me to thinking. Neither of us has anybody to speak on our behalf if we are unable to advocate for ourselves and wind up in the hospital, right?"

Marion gave a slight nod.

"When we die, our social security will go back to the government. What a waste, right?"

Another small nod.

"We already have a family, a daughter, a sort-of-son-in-law, even our new soul sister, Aunt Dot," she said.

"Aren't you forgetting one minor issue? I'm not a lesbian." Marion said. "I mean if I marry a woman, doesn't that make me a lesbian?"

"No, it just makes you married," Amanda replied. "Being a lesbian makes you a lesbian," she added pragmatically.

"This is the most unconventional thing you've come up with yet. At least, it's legal now."

"Is that a yes?" Amanda raised her eyebrows.

"No. It's not a 'yes.' But, it's not exactly a 'no,'" Marion said. "Give me some time to think about this. You sprung it on me out of the blue."

Every couple of hours, Marion interrupted Amanda with another concern.

"Nothing would change in our relationship if we got married, right?"

"Well, we should probably move into one bedroom," Amanda replied. She watched Marion pale. "I'm *kidding*. Geez. Nope, no changes."

And later, "What if you fall in lust again and want to start dating?"

"I assure you; I am quite beyond that. Would you be jealous?" she asked as an afterthought, just a little pleased with the idea.

"No. I'd be afraid."

"Ah, yes. I think we both know from my brief relationship history that my person-picker is broken."

"You mean the narcissist, the heroin addict, and the serial killer?" Marion ticked them off on her fingers to which Amanda gave a sheepish grin and shrugged.

"Um, what does that make me, then?" Marion asked.

"Not my type?" Amanda said.

———

It was a warm September afternoon. They stood on a hillside of golden grass under a white wooden arch laced with purple wisteria and blue morning glories.

The sky was robin-egg blue, and the refrain from Pachelbel's Canon played on the cello by their neighbor John, drifted on the air.

Marion wore an antique-white lace dress. Amanda's white linen pantsuit was a carryover from a cruise they'd taken a year prior. Both carried corsages of white roses and purple iris.

Officiating the ceremony was a former Universal Unitarian minister, now the pagan High Priestess of the Church of All Womyn.

In attendance and as witnesses to this somewhat less than holy event, were Chase, Toby, and Madison Bright.

Also by Jo Lauer

An Unlikely Trio

Best Laid Plans

Gone Awry

Returning: A Collection of Stories

Second Floor Front

It's in the Ink

Available through Amazon.

Photograph by Sara Frampton

Jo Lauer, a transplant from the Midwest, is a psychotherapist in Sonoma County, California. Her articles and essays have appeared in *Sacred Hoop*, *Psychology Today*, *Journal of Clinical Activities, Assignments & Handouts in Psychotherapy Practice*, *Tiny Light*, *Moondance*, *GRIT*, *In the Family*, and *Sonoma County Women's Voices*. She has published a novella, *Waltzing with the Azaleas*.

Her story, "Quilt of Souls," appears in the *Vintage Voices 2010 Redwood Writers Anthology: Words Poured Out*. Her essay, "She," appears in *Potpourri for and About Women (2010)*. Her essay, "Oak Tree Intermediary," was performed by Petaluma Readers Theatre (2011).

Please visit her website at *www.jolauer.com*.

www.ingramcontent.com/pod-product-compliance
Lightning Source LLC
Chambersburg PA
CBHW071312200626
46813CB00015B/1592